BEYOND THE LOCH

A SEVEN WARDENS PREQUEL

LAURA GREENWOOD

SKYE MACKINNON

Peryton Press

CONTENTS

Adventure waits beyond the loch...

Before she became known as the Loch Ness Monster, Nessie was nothing more than a simple kelpie with big dreams.

When her chance for adventure comes, she grabs it with both hands, sending her to the depths of the ocean and mountain peaks. Though none of that compares to what awaits her heart when she meets a human who still believes in magic...

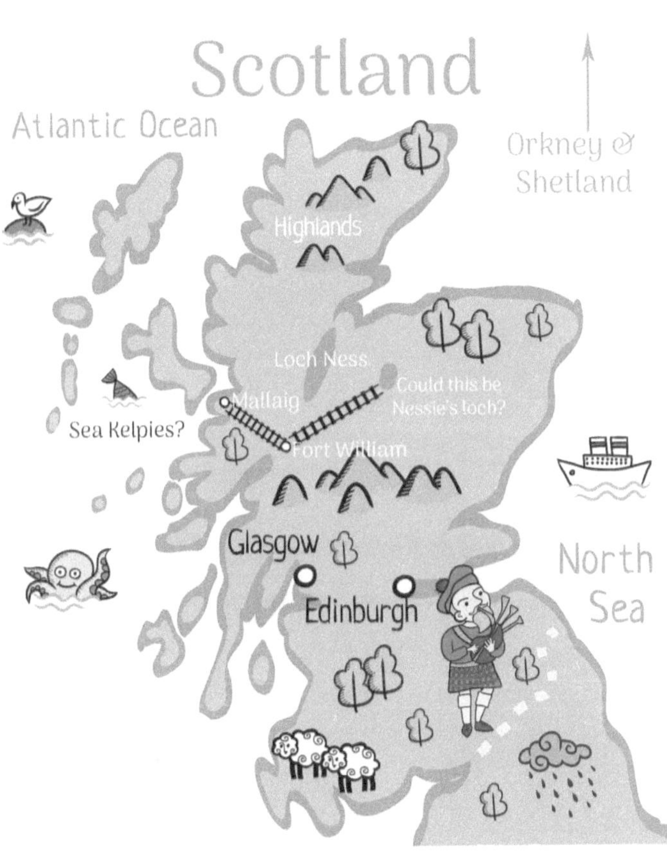

Scotland
Atlantic Ocean
Orkney &
Shetland
Highlands
Loch Ness
Could this be
Nessie's loch?
Mallaig
Sea Kelpies?
Fort William
Glasgow
North
Sea
Edinburgh

PROLOGUE

Nessie roared at the fisherman, his hook embedded in her flank. She pushed her back against the boat's keel, making it wobble dangerously from side to side. The man screamed and clung to the railing.

She needed to shift back and pull the hook out, otherwise, she'd accidentally bring the vessel down into the depths. The consequences weren't any she wanted to face. It would probably mean her time visiting the sea kelpies was well and truly done. They wouldn't keep her around if she broke the number one rule they all shared.

Don't let humans see a shifted kelpie.

It should have been simple, yet here she was trapped on a fisherman's line.

Again.

She took a deep breath, filling her lungs with the

salty sting of sea water. Forcing her muscles to relax, she pulled her human self to the surface. Bones cracked and skin tore as pain lanced through her entire body. The gods had been cruel when they'd created kelpies. Neither of their forms could survive long in the other's environment and yet the change between the two was so painful it was almost prohibitive.

Cold seeped through her entire human form and she paddled her legs frantically, hoping it would be enough to keep her afloat and away from harm. Reaching for the hook still embedded in her, Nessie gritted her teeth and yanked it out. She held back a scream, glad her soft human skin had let the hook be removed easier than her tough hide would have.

Shouts sounded from the boat above and she glanced up. Men were pointing at her, no doubt thinking she was a stowaway who'd fallen overboard. She couldn't let them pull her out of the sea, not when it would mean her losing any chance of finding out the sea kelpies' secrets. They'd hinted at having so many, and yet had told her none. If she could just stay with them a little longer then maybe they'd start to let her in on some of them. She'd heard rumours that they knew how to make the shift between forms less painful, and she'd definitely take that knowledge if she could.

Without any other choice, she sucked in a breath

and dived under the water. She couldn't shift again while they were watching, not when it risked revealing her kind to the world. At least the legends about mermaids made sense to Nessie now. Sailors had no doubt seen other creatures like kelpies or beithirs shifting and thought they were seeing beautiful sea maidens. The fools.

Her foot caught on something but she tried to ignore it, swimming on as hard as she could, even as her lungs began to burn. This body wasn't built to withstand the pressure of the water around her. Even so, she needed to push on. If she didn't, she'd never get back to the sea kelpie dome.

Pushing her hand through the water, she found the hook had caught her foot, leaving her without a chance of escape. She tried not to let panic take her. If it did, she'd end up shifted and in even more trouble than she already was. Even as she tried to swim, she was dragged backwards by the net she could sense around her. She hadn't stayed out of trouble enough and she was about to pay for it. If only she had some kind of sharp implement on her, then she'd be able to cut herself free and wouldn't risk the exposure of her species.

The urge to shift increased again but she pushed it down. The dangers were too great. Her lungs began to burn from the effort of holding her breath. There had to be an easier way to swim underwater when she wasn't in kelpie form. Maybe a partial shift?

Black spots swam across her vision at the effort. If she had to guess, she'd say she didn't have the energy to shift again, even if she wanted to.

Cold air hit her drenched skin, causing her to erupt in goosebumps. Nessie stopped the struggle and collapsed against the side of the net, letting it carry the bulk of her weight. If they were going to catch her like a common fish, then she wasn't going to make life easier for them.

She crashed onto the deck, the impact making her vision fail again. She sensed rather than saw the men crowding around her and wished she had the energy to cover herself. Forcing her eyes open, she looked up at them. There were four. Three blobs she'd never seen before and one who...

"You," he hissed, his eyes narrowing in hatred.

"Me," she croaked, a small smile spreading across her lips.

"Throw her back overboard," the man said to the others.

"We can't..."

She strained her ears to catch the rest of what the men were saying, but couldn't make out a single word of it before blackness fell once more...

ONE

One month earlier

She hated humans. Well, not hated them specifically, just where they lived. On land. She shuddered even just thinking about walking through that much air. She was going to miss the pressure of the water against her skin, the sound of the waves from far above, the smell of the weeds floating through the Loch.

Nessie loved her loch, despite all the things she'd said about leaving in the past few months. Yes, she wanted to explore and see the world, but she knew she'd also miss her home. Kelpies were able to live on land, but that didn't mean she'd enjoy it. Trouble was, to get to the sea, she had to travel over it. Her Loch wasn't connected to the ocean, so land it was.

She took one last breath, enjoying the sensation of water running through her gills, then began the shift. It was as painful as ever. Sometimes, she thought that the pain grew worse the older she got. She couldn't remember it being this painful when she first started shifting as a child. Her bones cracked as they became shorter and her skin burned as her scales disappeared. Then her lungs began to scream in agony. That was always the worst bit. She squeezed her eyes shut and focused on why she was doing this. Travel. Explore. Meet the sea kelpies. Make new friends. Expand her horizon. And, best of all: Get away from her overprotective mother. She remembered the knowing wink her father had given her when she'd told them that she was going to go travelling. He was well aware of how suffocating her mother's love could be sometimes.

The pain ebbed away and she broke the surface, taking a deep breath. The air was cool and refreshing, filling her lungs in a different way than when she pulled oxygen from water with her gills. It felt more intense somehow. Full of smells and life.

Slowly, she waded to the edge of the loch, dragging her waterproof bag behind her. It held one set of human clothes that another kelpie had given her. Nessie hadn't even considered that humans might find it strange if she walked fully naked into their village. The few times she'd left the water before, she'd stayed on the banks of the loch, playing with the pebbles lining it. She'd never ventured into the village that the other kelpies had told her about.

Her mother had offered to accompany her - well, it hadn't been so much an offer as a threat - but luckily, Nessie's father had convinced his wife that this was their daughter's big adventure, to be experienced without parents and relatives.

She slipped into the clothes, realising that the trousers were far too big for her. She was going to need to find some rope to keep them in place. It felt strange to have fabric so close to her skin. Her friend had offered her a pair of jeans, but those looked so tight and oppressive that she'd opted for looser fabric instead.

Her t-shirt was a little wide as well, but she quite liked it that way. Her nipples pushed against the cotton and she realised that maybe she should have taken the bra the other kelpie had shown her. Oh well, it was too late for that. A shiver ran over her skin. It was colder than she'd expected. She was going to have to get herself a jacket.

Once she'd realised that Nessie would go on her own, her mother had given her a bunch of human money. It was in her waterproof bag together with some other basic supplies. Her mother had said that it would be enough to last her a few months, but Nessie wasn't sure how much it was exactly. They didn't have money down in the Loch. They bartered and traded, but with so few kelpies left, they had no need for hard currency.

Nessie put on her shoes - they didn't quite fit, yet another thing for her shopping list - and headed up the overgrown path leading to the village. There were several human settlements dotted around the loch, but this one was the biggest. From here, she'd be able to take a train towards the sea. Or a bus, but the train sounded a lot more exciting.

After only ten minutes of walking through the dense heather brush, she saw the village in the distance. It was early evening and the light was slowly beginning to fade. She was planning to spend the night here, buy some clothes and food, and then move on the next day. She'd been told that there was a quaint little bed and breakfast in the village that many kelpies had visited before. The owners were distant relatives, even though they'd long lost the ability to shift over the generations.

It was as good a place as any to start. Some of the older kelpies had planned their trips before going on land, but she wasn't the type. Something about planning every moment of the adventure took the fun out of it for her. She wanted the experience, the chance of it all going completely wrong. Maybe she'd meet someone who'd turn her world upside down and back to front. While she didn't want to admit that was part of the draw of coming to land, it was.

Her mother had been pushing her towards the various male kelpies her age for the past few months and she was fed up of it. She'd known them all for so long that she was sure she didn't want anything to do with any of them other than the obligatory pleasantries which couldn't be avoided.

She pushed open the heavy wooden door and stepped into the inn. The air was thick with the stench of roasting meat, turning Nessie's stomach. She'd been brought up to avoid any kind of animal or fish products.

"Ah, you're here. We've been expecting you," a woman greeted her.

"Hello," Nessie responded. "I'm Vanessa." Her voice shook from the nerves she didn't want to admit having. She wasn't this kind of kelpie. She'd been brought up to stand proud and hold her ground, all others should bend to her. It might be a little arrogant of her, but it was better to be on top than sidelined.

"Yes, your mother wrote ahead. But you need to come with me. We can't let you be seen in a man's getup." She closed a hand around Nessie's wrist and pulled her deeper into the inn.

"What do you-"

"Just because we're in the middle of nowhere, it doesn't mean you can get away with wearing men's clothes. Where's your corset? Your skirts?"

"My what?" Nessie's eyes widened. The older kelpie had told her she'd be fine in the clothes she'd given Nessie. Why was that suddenly not the case?

The woman sighed and shut the door behind them before turning to search through a wooden chest. "You're not wearing women's clothes, Vanessa. You'll never fit in if you don't." She threw several items of clothing on the small bed while muttering more to herself.

"Oh. This is what I was..."

"You kelpies are all the same." She stood up and turned around, putting her hands on her hips and studying Nessie intently. "Especially the highborn."

Nessie didn't respond. High and low born didn't really exist in kelpie society, but she knew that, with her family, this woman was almost right about her place in it. Not that she was about to admit that aloud. Her mother had made her swear she wouldn't reveal her full identity to anyone from outside the Loch.

"And I wouldn't use Vanessa either, it's not a very Scottish name. You'll only draw attention to yourself."

"Alright." Nessie nodded, knowing what else she could say. "Thank you for your help."

"You're welcome. Now put those on and then come join us for a meal. I'm sure you've been told you have a free night here too. In the morning, you'll need to move on."

"Thank you," Nessie repeated. She'd been told all of this before she'd left the loch, but it was good to have a refresher for how things would go now she was actually faced with them.

"We can't offer you shelter on your way back to the Loch."

"I'm aware, thank you."

"Good. I shall see you in a moment." The woman left the room, shutting the door firmly behind her. It was only after a moment or two that Nessie realised she didn't know the woman's name.

Ignoring that odd behaviour, Nessie looked through the clothing on the bed, trying to sort out what she had to wear in what order. It all looked somewhat straightforward to put on, even if a little uncomfortable in some places. She certainly wasn't looking forward to the half-corset which was among the pile. She was lucky the thing came with the instructions on how to put it on, no doubt hand-drawn by the woman who'd given her the clothes in the first place. It wasn't anything like any of the clothing they had underwater and Nessie imagined there would be a lot of confused kelpies at this stage.

She dressed as quickly as possible and wet her

face. It was probably unnecessary, but her host seemed like the kind of woman who would appreciate the gesture more than anything else.

With skirts now falling to her ankles and a shirt buttoned up to her chin, she felt like some kind of doll. Hopefully, the woman wasn't serious about this style of clothing. She'd take the weird looseness of the other outfit over this one but for now, it was what she needed to wear. At least the boots were comfortable, even if they would take a little bit of getting used to. She'd much rather be walking around barefoot as she did in the kelpie palace though.

"Sit. Eat," the woman instructed the moment she left the small bedroom.

Not knowing what else to do, Nessie sat on the worn wooden bench and pulled a bowl of soup towards her. She took a spoonful before letting it drop back into the liquid with a soft plopping sound.

The woman sighed and almost threw the bread at Nessie. "Don't worry, there's no meat in it. I know what your kind are like about that." She didn't wait for Nessie to respond and went back to doing whatever she was before. "No need to turn up your nose about it," she muttered, surely too low for a human to hear. Not for a kelpie though.

Nessie ignored it, knowing there wasn't much else she could do at this stage. Tomorrow, she'd set off and leave the inn behind. Until then, she was dependent on the woman's hospitality and she wasn't going to do anything to compromise that.

TWO

Nessie left the bed and breakfast as soon as the sun had risen behind the hills in the distance. She muttered a quick goodbye to the landlady, who was rummaging in the kitchen and slipped out of the door.

Her first night on land had been restless and she couldn't wait to move on. Sleeping on a hard mattress without the sound of the water had been hard. Her body was achy, probably because she'd never stayed in her human form for this long. The other kelpies had assured her that there was no need for her to shift to kelpie form regularly to survive, but she didn't like the dry feeling of her human skin. She was going to try and get to the sea without too many delays.

The train station was quiet and deserted. The little ticket office was unoccupied. Hopefully, she'd be able to get a ticket on the train. Nessie was itching to try the whole paying with money thing. It sounded exciting, counting the right coins into the conductor's hand.

She checked the timetable, seeing in relief that the times the other kelpies had told her were still correct. The train was going to arrive in a few minutes, so she didn't bother sitting down on one of the rusty old benches.

An old man hobbled towards her from the other end of the platform.

"Beautiful wee morning, aye?" he said in broad Scots, but it wasn't a question. He took a deep puff from his pipe and then ignored Nessie.

She shrugged at the peculiarity of humans. Back in the loch, she'd have started a conversation, but here, she wasn't quite sure about the customs. She stayed quiet, watching the hands of the station clock move slower than should be possible.

Finally, the train arrived, steam billowing from the locomotive. It came to a halt with a loud screech. She let the old man approach the iron monster first, watching the way he managed to pull open one of the heavy doors.

It was nice and warm inside and she quickly found an empty compartment. There were almost no people on the train. She was glad about that. She didn't know what humans talked about when they met as strangers. If they even talked at all. She knew everyone in the loch, there were no strangers there. When they had visitors from other lochs or the sea, others had met them already and would tell her about them. She'd never been in such a situation before.

She shook her head, admonishing herself for all those negative thoughts. This was the big adventure she'd always dreamed of and she was supposed to enjoy it.

With another screech, the train set into motion. Nessie could smell the coal that powered the engines. It was a strangely calming scent that carried her off to sleep after only a few minutes.

"Is this seat free?"

A deep, calm voice roused her from her sleep. Nessie blinked a few times, bringing the man who'd woken her into focus. It was a young man, maybe in his mid-twenties, with a dark tweed suit, sharp green eyes and very ginger hair. If he'd been wearing a kilt, he'd have been just what she'd imagined a Scottish human to look like.

"Yes, it's free," she muttered sleepily, clearing her throat.

The man smiled. "Thank you."

Nessie sat up a little straighter and smoothed her skirt. Suddenly, she was feeling a little self-conscious.

The young man heaved his large suitcase onto the overhead locker and then sat down on the bench opposite her, putting both a newspaper and a hip flask on the seat next to him.

"Travelling far?" he asked, looking right at Nessie. His gaze was intense as if he was trying to see more than just her outside. Like he was trying to see into her soul. In a way, it was creepy, but at the same time, he seemed trustworthy. Nice. A gentleman.

"To the sea," she replied, not quite wanting to give him too much information. "What about you?"

He smiled again. "To Fort William. I've got some business to do there."

"Is that far?" she asked before realising that she should probably know that - if she was human. She didn't know much about the human towns dotted around the Scottish landscape. She did know every single body of water though, no matter how small. She had other priorities.

"Usually it's two hours from here," he replied, "but I've heard there's a tree on the line further West that they're trying to remove. We might be delayed today."

Luckily, Nessie wasn't in any hurry. The man looked a little annoyed though.

"Will you be late for something?" she asked.

He nodded. "I have a meeting with my uncle's lawyer. It's going to be boring but I need to be on time. I can't risk making a bad impression."

"I'm sure you couldn't make a bad impression," Nessie said before she could stop herself.

He raised an eyebrow. "Thank you, I guess."

The man reached out a hand. "I'm Jonas."

"Nessie," she replied, just about managing not to say Vanessa. She wasn't sure if the woman at the B&B had been right about Vanessa not being a Scottish name, but she didn't want to risk it. She was sure that she was going to do enough blunders that could expose her.

"Nice to meet you."

He smiled, then reached for his newspaper. She was a bit confused. He'd introduced himself, now he was going to read the paper and ignore her? She wasn't going to let him do that. She was bored and he'd woken her from her little nap. It was only fair that he had to talk to her.

"Are you going to stay the night in Fort William?" she asked and he looked up from his paper.

"It depends on how long the meeting is going to last. It might be half an hour or three hours, who knows. I don't know much about what's going to happen."

Nessie was getting more and more curious, but she wasn't sure how much she was able to ask without seeming impolite. But then she decided that she didn't care. She was never going to see this young man again, so why not satisfy her curiosity.

"What's the meeting about?" she asked.

A slight frown appeared on Jonas's smooth forehead, but then he smiled again, a little sadly this time. Nessie realised how pretty his smile was, even though it had a slightly melancholic edge.

"My grandfather died a month ago and today I'm going to find out what he put in his will."

She swallowed hard. Damn, she'd put her foot right in it.

"I'm so sorry," she muttered.

He shrugged. "We weren't close, but since my father's no longer alive, I have to attend. I guess it gives me an excuse to get out and about a bit. I've not been to Fort William in ages."

"I've never been," Nessie admitted. "Is it nice there?"

He shrugged again and she noticed how his chest muscles moved beneath his tight suit. Was she actually ogling a human?

"It's quite pretty," he replied. "But if I'm having to stay there overnight, I might go up Ben Nevis tomorrow."

"Scotland's highest mountain," Nessie said, proud that she knew that.

His eyes lit up. "Yes. Do you know it well?"

"I'm sorry, I don't. Just the story of Mary McCloud." Nessie didn't want to meet his gaze in fear of the disappointment she might find there.

"Don't be sorry. It's hard to find people with an interest in mountaineering. Especially beautiful young women."

A blush rose to Nessie's cheeks. She hadn't expected to find a human man so charming. There was a small chance he wasn't as human as he seemed but if that was the case, he surely would have called her out on her own lack of humanity.

"It sounds like a fascinating sport, I've just never had a chance to try it," she told him. The latter part of her statement was even true. She hadn't tried it before, but neither had she really had the urge. For this man though....she could change her mind for this man.

"What's the legend you've heard? I'm not sure I'm familiar with that one." He took out a small notebook and pencil and readied himself to write it down.

"Do you always take notes when you're talking to people?" she asked, nodding towards the page.

"Only when the other person has something interesting to say," he responded. "The story?"

"I'm sure there are several versions. The one I know is about two clans at war."

"Do you know their names?" He was paying rapt

attention like she was telling him the most interesting thing he could possibly have imagined.

"I think the clan leaders were called Angus McDonald and Robert McCloud." She thought back over all the history lessons she'd suffered through back in the Loch.

"And where does Mary fit in?" His expression reminded her of a curious kelpie child, one that hadn't heard this story hundreds of times before.

"It was custom for the chief's wife to go up Ben Nevis before a battle and bring down lucky heather for the clansmen. But when Mary reached the top, instead of doing that, she began to cry. The ghost of a Highlander appeared to her and asked her why she was crying. She told him there'd been enough bloodshed and she didn't want to see anymore. The Highlander assured her that if she brought him some haggis the next morning, there wouldn't be any bloodshed to worry about." She paused in her story and glanced out of the window, taking in the vast green fields they passed. Scotland truly was beautiful. Outside the Loch as well as beneath it.

"I wonder what a ghost wanted haggis for," Jonas mused, tapping his pencil against his chin as he stared at the notes on his page.

"The same thing all ghosts want food for. To fuel them." Nessie shrugged. She didn't know where the human misconception that ghosts didn't need feeding had come from, but it was safe to say they were rather dense on the situation.

"Have you ever had haggis?" His question surprised her. She'd have thought he'd ask something more obvious about the ghosts, but that didn't seem to be the direction he was going in.

"No. I don't eat meat. Have you?"

He nodded vigorously. "It's mother's favourite. I've had to endure many meals containing haggis." He pulled up his upper lip, disgust painted for everyone to see.

Nessie giggled. "Maybe you should avoid meat too, it makes avoiding haggis a lot easier," she suggested.

"I imagine it does. Is there more to your story?" He gave her an expectant look.

She smiled in response. Of all the things she'd imagined when she'd decided to get on the train, this response wasn't one of them. She loved the fact she could have an informative conversation with someone. And that she didn't sound uneducated while she did it. Far from it if what the woman at the inn had said. It almost sounded like women weren't supposed to be able to hold educated conversations with men.

"Yes. Mary returned to her husband and his men and told them what had happened. They didn't believe her, though I'm not sure if that's because she was a woman or because they didn't believe in ghosts..."

"Both of which are ridiculous reasons to disbelieve someone," Jonas muttered, making a quick note in his book. "Please, go on."

"But Mary wasn't the kind to be put off just because people didn't believe her and she made up some haggis anyway. She set off up Ben Nevis again and gave the haggis to the ghost, even though she couldn't see him."

"And did the ghost stop the bloodshed?"

"He did." Nessie nodded enthusiastically. "When Mary returned to her husband, he told her a messenger had arrived and that Angus McDonald had died and his son had taken his place as chief."

"Did his son have a name?" Jonas asked.

Nessie racked her brain, trying to remember what she'd been told. "His name was Jonas," she whispered.

He chuckled. "You're making that up."

She shook her head. "I promise, I'm not. That's what my history tutor always told me."

"It's unbelievable how things connect sometimes."

"Or maybe your name reminded me of the story on some level," she suggested. "Why are you so interested in stories about Ben Nevis?"

"Promise you won't laugh?" He closed his book

and rested it on his knees, a serious expression settling on his face.

"I'll try not to," she responded. "Please tell me?" She crossed her fingers and hoped she wouldn't end up breaking her promise. She didn't want to hurt the man who'd been so nice to her since the moment he'd sat down.

"I'm trying to find a ghost," he admitted.

She raised an eyebrow. "You are?"

"Yes. I'm convinced there's more to the world than meets the eye and if I can find one, then I'll know for sure."

"Does that make you a ghost hunter?" she asked.

"I suppose it does," he admitted. "Though I hadn't thought of myself like that."

"Where are you hunting for a ghost next?" she asked.

"Now you've told me this, I'm thinking Ben Nevis."

THREE

She watched as the sun yawned, stretched, then slowly rose above the mist-covered hills in the distance. She felt just as tired as she imagined the sun to be. She'd not slept well, thoughts of Jonas incessantly interrupting her dreams. Now she was waiting for the same man who'd caused her to toss from side to side all night.

Yesterday, they'd decided that they were going to climb the mountain together, no matter whether Jonas's meeting would overrun or not. She found it a little strange that the young man had invited her to come along - after all, they'd only spent a few hours on the train together talking - but she didn't want to say no to this adventure. She'd never been hiking before, but it sounded rather romantic. Peeking through the thick cloud cover, reaching towards the sun, viewing the world from a higher angle. Yes, it was going to be fun, she was sure of that. Now Jonas just had to hurry up. She didn't want to freeze in the cool morning air.

She rubbed her arms. She was wearing outdoor clothes that the lady in the shop had assured her were suited for climbing Ben Nevis. Nonetheless, Nessie wished the woman hadn't refused to sell her trousers. Again, she was stuck wearing a skirt, although this one was shorter and wider than the one she'd worn before. Underneath, she wore thick woollen tights and walking boots. They were a little tight but she'd been told that the leather would soften over time. She really hoped she hadn't been too gullible during her first shopping experience. It had all been a little overwhelming, but she'd enjoyed the thrill of spending money. It was fascinating how everyone seemed to be addicted to giving or receiving those metal coins. She'd never really understood the purpose while still living in the Loch, but here, it made sense. People didn't know each other; bartering would have been much harder. Besides, Nessie didn't have anything here that she could barter with.

"Good morning!" a voice shouted cheerily from behind her. She turned and grinned as she saw Jonas half-walking, half-running towards her. They'd agreed to meet at the edge of town because when they'd separated at the train station, Nessie hadn't known yet where she was going to spend the night.

"Beautiful day for a hike!" Jonas called cheerily, panting from obviously having hurried to get there in time.

Nessie nodded towards the clouds covering the mountains in the distance as if to challenge his words. The sun was already losing its battle, giving way to a thick layer of mist.

"You don't want it to be too hot when you walk," he explained. "It makes you sweaty and dehydrated. No, weather like this is perfect. No rain, but cool and dry. Hopefully, the clouds will clear enough by the time we get to the top. The view is supposed to be amazing."

She supposed that made sense. She didn't like it when it got too hot. Granted, it rarely did, this was Scotland, after all, but still. She was a water creature and preferred rain over sun that burned her scales.

"Have you been up there before?" she asked, watching him as he pulled an old, tattered map from his backpack.

"Aye, many times, but mostly when I was a child. It's been at least five years since I last went up the mountain. Never thought I'd do it with a beautiful woman."

She grimaced. He was calling her beautiful far too often. She wasn't used to anyone doing that. Besides her mother, and that was different, very different indeed.

"Let's go," she replied, distracting herself from his flattery. "How long will it take us?"

He winked at her. "That depends on how fast you can walk."

She gave him a challenging grin. "Faster than you."

Before he'd even closed his backpack again, she walked off, following the old wooden sign clearly stating 'Ben Nevis Mountain Track'. It wasn't possible really to misinterpret that.

With a chuckle, Jonas followed her and quickly fell into step to her left, easily matching her pace. Frowning, she walked a little faster, adding a tiny bit of kelpie strength to her strides. A muscle twitched along the hard edge of Jonas's jaw, but again he managed to keep up with her. She smiled to herself. She wasn't going to overdo it. She knew she looked like a young, innocent woman and Jonas might have had a heart attack if he knew that she could topple one of the trees surrounding them. Even when she was in her human form, she could access her kelpie strength. Her magic, too, but that was much harder to hide.

Jonas began to whistle a tune Nessie didn't know, but she liked it. She listened as they walked. The path gradually became steeper and rockier. They were still surrounded by forest so they didn't have the grandiose views she'd been promised, but they'd only been walking for half an hour.

They didn't talk much, but it was a friendly, companionable silence. When they reached a grassy outcrop, Jonas took off his backpack and handed Nessie a bottle. She'd brought her own, but he didn't seem to realise that. Thinking it impolite to refuse, she took a big gulp of water before giving the bottle back to him. Their fingers touched for a split second but it was enough to send a pleasant shiver along Nessie's skin. So that's what it felt like to be touched by a human man. Did they all tingle like that? Would every man give her goosebumps? That would get highly distracting. Hopefully, it was just windchill.

Jonas met her eyes and then his hand was on hers again, holding her in place, his fingers warm on her own. He didn't say anything, just kept staring into her eyes as if he was searching for something.

A tiny fly flew into Nessie's eye and she couldn't help but blink, ending that strange moment. While she was rubbing her eye, Jonas stepped back as if he'd finally noticed that they'd been standing close, very close. From what Nessie knew of human customs, it had been far too close for two unmarried strangers of the opposite sex. Still, she didn't mind. It was all part of the adventure.

Jonas cleared his throat. "Want to stay here for a bit or shall we continue?"

Nessie looked around, searching for the sun.

"I think it's clearing up a little," she muttered. "Maybe we better get going so we don't miss the sunshine at the top."

The young man nodded. "Good thinking. I can't wait to show you the view. You'll be as mind blown as I was the first time I climbed this mountain."

After a while, the forest gave way to a rocky slope, interrupted by small streams and zigzag curves. Nessie was loving it. The fresh air, the strain in her legs, good company. It was much better than she'd imagined.

"What got you into ghost hunting?" she asked once the question had occurred to her. It wasn't that she was bored with the silence as they walked, more that she was curious to hear more. And to work out how close to the supernatural he'd actually gotten. As far as she knew, she wasn't supposed to reveal what she was to any humans, so she made the assumption that other races were told the same when they went out into the world. But where did that leave Jonas? Were there other humans who'd come as close as he had to the real truth of the world?

"A girl I knew at university in Saint Andrews swore she'd seen a ghost. I dismissed it at first but curiosity got the better of me. I spent hours in the library looking into ghost sightings and other supernatural things. The more I read, the more convinced I became that they were real. If I'd had my way, I'd have written my thesis on it, but no one would approve the mixing of science with the supernatural."

"That's a shame," she muttered, not meaning it at all. It was better for the supernatural community as a whole.

"It is. I only want to look for more in the world. There's so much wonder yet to be discovered."

She didn't respond. She couldn't. Not when he had no idea what his discoveries would do if they spread out into the wider world.

"What do you do?" he asked.

"Do?"

"When you're not hiking up mountains with complete strangers, I mean."

A stone dropped in Nessie's stomach. How did she answer that one? She didn't do anything in particular in the Loch. She was the daughter of upper-class kelpies, she didn't need to work.

"I study," she answered, hoping humans let women be educated. Jonas might have met a girl at university, but that didn't mean she studied there too. Hopefully, she wasn't putting her foot in it.

"Oh, where?"

"A small university. No one's ever heard of it." She

shrugged and thought about the best way to change the subject. It would be easier if she avoided talking about her home, then she wouldn't have to think of lies to cover up the truth. "Do you really think we'll find the ghost of a Highlander?" Bringing ghosts up seemed like a sure fire way of distracting him.

"I hope so. Luckily, I brought my camera, just in case."

"You can catch them on film?" Worry gnawed away within her. Photographic evidence of something out of this world wasn't going to end well.

"Not very well, but enough for me to be able to study it," he responded.

"I suppose something is better than nothing."

"Exactly."

They lapsed back into silence and continued up the mountain. For Nessie, it was easy going but she could hear Jonas panting next to her. The thinner air and hard climb were clearly taking more of a toll on him than on her, but she didn't want to offer any help in case he learned something incriminating. She'd thought it would be easy to conceal her powers, but now not so much.

"Do you have any brothers and sisters?" he blurted after a while.

"No, you?"

"No. I'm an only child. Probably one of the reasons I got into hunting for something more."

"Was it lonely?" She wasn't sure what prompted her to ask. There were so many kelpie children about that she'd always had enough people around to play with and talk to.

"I guess? I used to tell myself stories when I was a kid."

"About ghosts?" she prompted.

"And princesses, knights, King Arthur..."

"Who?" That wasn't a legend she'd ever heard before.

"You don't know about Arthur and the Knights of the Round Table?" Shock marred his voice.

"I'm sorry, I don't. Will you tell me about them?"

"Of course." He proceeded to regale her with tales of the King and his knights, the adventures thrilling her but also sounding vaguely familiar.

"I've heard some of those before," she said after he'd finished. "But under a different title."

"Oh?" He glanced at her, a look of intrigue on his face.

"The stories I've heard like that are all about the fourth set of the Seven Wardens."

"Seven Wardens?" he echoed.

"Yes, seven humans who are chosen to become guardians of the Staran throughout the world. The leader of the fourth set of Wardens was called Arthur. I believe he was the Earth Warden."

"You're speaking in tongues now." He gave a short

chuckle but she could tell from his tone that he was intrigued.

"I'm not meaning to. The Wardens are a common legend where I'm from. Arthur is just part of that."

"Do you have a Guinevere in those legends too?" He held out his hand to stop her from walking and handed her the water bottle again.

She took a deep drink, thinking back through the legends she knew. "Yes, I believe she was the Ice Warden in our tales." She handed him the bottle back and he took a drink.

"And the Wardens are responsible for..?" he prompted as they set off again.

"Keeping the supernatural pathways around the world open," she responded, wondering if she was skating too close to the truth of the world at the moment.

"There are supernatural pathways?" There was no need for her to see his eyes light up to know it had happened. He really loved this kind of thing.

"It's just a story told to kids, I don't think we can take it literally."

His shoulders drooped and a part of her longed to reach out and touch him, to reassure him that all wasn't lost. That the things he wanted to exist in the world really did and he was closer to one than he thought. Though she wasn't sure what his response would be if he discovered she was actually a kelpie.

"Are you sure there isn't any proof for it?" he asked, the eagerness still coming through his words.

"I'm sure there's always some truth in all of the legends. But I'm not sure how much in this case." She wasn't even lying. She'd never met a Warden and had no proof they were real. Though in all likelihood, there was a lot of truth in these ones. No matter what reiteration, a lot of the facts about the Wardens stayed the same, no matter who was doing the telling.

"Where did you grow up to hear such legends?" he asked between shallow breaths. She slowed down a little more, not wanting him to get too exhausted by trying to keep up with her. "I've been trying to place your accent."

She shrugged. "A small village in the Highlands, you wouldn't have heard of it." She looked around, desperate for a distraction. He was asking too many questions and she wasn't sure how much she could tell him. She knew the people in the villages surrounding the Loch spoke with a different accent than she did, so she couldn't give him their names. This was all rather complicated.

Luckily, the distraction came in form of a thick root that she overlooked. She tripped and fell to the ground, her hands painfully hitting the rough stone. She cursed under her breath even though it didn't really hurt that much. It was mainly her pride that was in pain.

"Are you alright?"

Jonas stretched out a hand and pulled her back on her feet. She rubbed her hands against her dress, cleaning away both dust and sprinkles of blood.

"Yes, I'm fine," she said quickly as his brow began to furrow. Was he actually concerned about her? They'd only just met. She wasn't used to men that weren't her guards being so caring. "Let's continue or we might miss the sun."

She nodded towards the thin sliver of sunlight that was barging its way through thick layers of clouds. It seemed the sun was finally getting stronger in its battle against the darkness. Nessie smiled at how dramatic that sounded in her mind.

They started walking again, neither of them saying much. Nessie enjoyed breathing in the clean mountain air. She'd not enjoyed all the smells and stink of Fort William. Up here, the air tasted much better. Even better than the air at the Loch.

"Wait," Jonas suddenly said and put a hand on her shoulder, stopping her in her tracks. "I think I saw something."

She looked around, following his gaze. They'd reached a steep slope where a well-worn path was cut through boulders and scree. To their right, the drop-off was making Nessie queasy. It wasn't that the height was giving her trouble - in the Loch, she was often far away from the ground - it was the sheer amounts of empty air. It boggled her mind how that much air could stay in one place without being sucked into the sky. Yes, of course she knew all about physics and the atmosphere and all that stuff, but still, seeing it was very different from reading about it in a book back at kelpie school.

"Can you see him?" Jonas asked hesitantly, pointing towards the place where the path was curving around the mountain, disappearing behind a large boulder.

Nessie squeezed her eyes together, trying to see what he was talking about, but there was nothing.

"No," she replied truthfully. "What's there?"

The young man sighed. "Nothing, I guess. I thought I'd seen a man's shadow on the track. Must have been a trick of the light."

Nessie nodded. Must have been. She was convinced that if there was a ghost, she'd be able to see him too. It was more likely for her to see him than for the human.

Seeming a little deflated, Jonas began to walk again and Nessie followed him, feeling like she should somehow console him.

FOUR

The higher they climbed, the more beautiful the views became. Nessie was awestruck by the mountains surrounding them like old gentlemen who'd sat down to rest. Close to the summit, they passed a small group of hikers who all looked decidedly exhausted. Nessie, however, was brimming with energy. Walking up mountains was going to be her new favourite pastime.

After another very steep bit, they finally reached a rocky plateau. There were several stone cairns in the distance as well as a strange looking building clinging to the mountaintop.

"Did it say anywhere in your legend where the ghost appeared on Ben Nevis?" Jonas asked, making Nessie grimace behind his back. Why did he have to keep going on about it? She was trying to enjoy the view without having to make difficult decisions about how much to tell him. She really hoped the ghost was just a fairy tale.

"It just mentions the top," she replied carefully. "But you know legends can be vague. It could be the very tip of the summit or the general top of the mountain, who knows." She smiled at the frustration mirroring on his fine features. "Even if we don't see a ghost, this view totally makes it worth it, right?"

He nodded. "It does. I always say how beautiful it is up here, yet when I return, it's even more stunning than I could remember. It's like my mind isn't strong enough to record the majesty of mother nature."

She knew what he meant. The scenery was breathtaking, there was no better word for it. Nessie smiled at the feeling of the wind against her face, the smell of the fresh air, the view of what seemed the entirety of the Scottish Highlands. And she smiled at the knowledge that Jonas was by her side, her new human acquaintance. Her very first human friend, maybe.

"There are too many people here to see ghosts anyway," the young man muttered more to himself than to Nessie.

She agreed with him. There were scores of walkers spread out over the plateau, several of them taking pictures of each other. She'd read about cameras in the newspapers some of the kelpies had brought home, but she'd never actually had a chance to try one. Maybe Jonas might let her have a go, once he'd realised that there wasn't going to be a ghost.

"There!" he suddenly shouted and she suppressed a sigh. He was going to embarrass himself in front of all these people, some of whom were already curiously turning towards them.

When she looked at what he was pointing though, she couldn't help but gasp. There was a ghost, a real ghost, a ghost in the shape of a man wearing a kilt. She blinked several times but he didn't disappear as she'd hoped. The Highlander the story told of was real.

"Do you see him?" Jonas whispered in shock. He was clutching his hands, his eyes wide, fixed on the apparition.

Nessie stayed quiet, unsure of what to say. If she said yes, he'd be introduced to the supernatural and he was the kind of person who wouldn't simply stop once he'd seen one kind of being. After the ghost, he'd go hunting for other species, maybe even kelpies. She couldn't allow that to happen. His curiosity could be a danger for her kind and all supernatural beings.

She took one last look at the ghost, who was sitting on a large rock, his face turned towards the sun as if he was enjoying the warmth. He was mostly translucent but there were traces of colours remaining on his clothes. His kilt, especially, although it was too faint to recognise the tartan. He ignored the humans around him and she was rather grateful for that.

She steeled herself, then said as gently as she could, "No, I can't see anyone."

The ghost looked straight at her and chuckled. "I see how this is going to be," he said.

Nessie sighed. If the ghost was going to talk to her, then that was going to cause some problems. The chances of her responding by accident were fairly high and that seemed like it could get them all into trouble if she wasn't careful.

"Are you real?" Jonas asked.

"Real enough. But to learn more, you must follow." The ghost rose to his feet and disappeared into a wisp of smoke.

Ghosts and their nonsense. She didn't know how they'd managed to get by for as long as they had when they were this cryptic.

The wisp pointed down a small dirt path and she knew the ghost expected them to follow. More than that, she knew Jonas would want to. She just hoped that when the ghost made himself visible again, it would be away from quite so many people. Nothing looked crazier than talking to mid-air. But if two people were doing it...

Better not to think about that. It was bad enough that Jonas would learn that ghosts definitely existed.

They set off down the path, Nessie being careful to only respond to the man's movements and not the ghosts. She'd have to see him when he reappeared, of that, she had no doubt, but she couldn't suddenly look at him now without raising some kind of suspicion.

"I can't believe it. A real ghost!" He was almost bouncing down the path, all traces of the long walk up and the exhaustion it had caused had vanished. This was a man who could see his lifelong dream in front of him and knew it was about to become reality. Deep down, she knew she couldn't take that from him by pretending the ghost didn't exist.

They turned a corner and the side of the path disappeared completely, leaving a deep gash in the mountainside. Nessie gulped loudly. Even she didn't think she'd be able to survive if she fell off the path. Nevermind Jonas.

"Where are you taking us?" she muttered under her breath, only intending the ghost to hear.

It didn't reply. Not that she was surprised.

"Careful with your footing," Jonas warned her.

"I will be," she responded sweetly, not adding that he had more to worry about that she did. Kelpies had an excellent sense of balance and she was going to make the most out of it while on a dangerous path.

The wisp disappeared to the right and panic almost made itself known within her. She didn't want

Jonas in danger just because of a ghost's whim. That wasn't fair to him. Or to her for that matter.

Reaching where it had gone, she noticed the small entrance to a cave. They'd have to duck, but it was clearly big enough for the two of them to get into.

"I guess we're going in here," she said.

"I thought you couldn't see the ghost?" Jonas asked.

Nessie's eyes widened. She hadn't intended to let him know she'd been able to. "I couldn't, but I did see a shimmer of light that you seemed to be following."

The ghost's chuckle filled the air around her. It seemed to know she was lying, though she had no idea how he possibly could. Especially when he wasn't in the immediate vicinity.

Jonas nodded, clearly having believed her lie.

"Shall we?" he asked, waving towards the door.

"Might as well." She didn't wait for him to say anything else and ducked through the cave entrance.

After a couple of steps in complete darkness, the cave opened up and Nessie gasped at the view in front of her. Jewels twinkled in the walls in all colours, shapes, and sizes. Light bounced around, giving the cavern a mythical air.

"No one who sees this can say the supernatural isn't real," Jonas said when he reached her side.

She didn't have the heart to tell him the effect

was nothing to do with magic and everything to do with nature. Even if it wasn't made that way, there was a magic in the way the place looked. Ethereal came to mind as a description.

"Welcome to the Cavern of Lights," the ghost said, reappearing in his humanoid form, complete with kilt blowing in the non-existent wind.

"Thank you." Jonas took a step forward. "Why have you brought us here, wise one?"

The ghost gave him an odd look before starting to laugh once more. "Wise one? Where did this one grow up?"

Nessie's lips quirked up into a brief smile. It wasn't Jonas's fault he didn't know how to address ghosts, even if that made it more amusing for her.

"My name is Gilbert. I'll have none of this wise-one stuff."

"Gilbert?" Jonas echoed.

"Aye. Is my name not a good one?" Menace flashed behind the ghost's eyes. Nessie didn't know how serious it was. She'd never met a ghost before, but from everything she'd heard, they could be rather temperamental creatures.

"It's a very good name," Jonas responded. "It just wasn't what I expected."

"You should always expect the unexpected, that way nothing ever comes as a surprise."

"I'm not sure that's true," Nessie put in. "What if

the expected happens? If you're expecting the unexpected then the expected would surprise you. No?"

The ghost roared in laughter, filling the cavern with the sound as it bounced off the walls. "Now, now, I should have known better than to play word games with someone such as you. Aren't you a long way from your loch?" He raised an eyebrow.

Nessie's heart sank. She hoped he wouldn't say any more, she wasn't ready for Jonas to learn the truth about her and what she was. "Not as far as I could be."

"I met your sort once before, while I was alive mind. She came from the sea. Beautiful, charming, but with the anger of the seas in her veins. Not one anyone should want to cross. I suspect you're the same," he told her.

"I'm from inland," she countered.

"Means nought. Just because you have been something all your life, doesn't mean that it's what you're meant to be. The sea is where you'll find your answers." His eyes pierced into her, giving weight to his words.

Nessie gulped. Maybe she should heed his words. She'd left the Loch for an adventure, after all, it wasn't like she had a plan anyway.

"And what about me?" Jonas asked, having recovered from looking between them with a look of anger on his face. She was sure she'd have a lot of questions to answer after Gilbert had disappeared once more. At the moment, only Jonas's eagerness to talk to the ghost before he disappeared was keeping her safe.

Gilbert studied him for a moment, a look of concentration marring his brow. "You are hard to read. I see two paths. One ends sooner than I think you'd like. The other takes you down a dangerous path that you'll never return from."

"If one of them ends soon, surely that's the more dangerous path?" Nessie interrupted.

The ghost turned to her. "You think death is the most dangerous thing in the world?" He raised a ghostly eyebrow.

"It's the most permanent," she pointed out.

"Hardly." He ran a hand down his body in explanation.

She had to admit he was right. He didn't exactly support the hypothesis of death being the end. That was annoying.

"So death or danger are my options?" Jonas asked, not sounding as worried about it as Nessie would have liked considering they were talking about his future.

"Those are the paths I'm seeing, but all can still be changed. Human nature likes to change things even quicker than the unpredictable nature of the sea."

"Should I be going to the coast too?" Jonas asked.

"Whatever gave you that idea?" Gilbert seemed genuinely taken aback by the question.

"You mentioned the sea for Nessie, and now again for me, I just thought..."

"I cannot tell either of you where you should go. All I can do is tell you what I see when I look at the two of you. Such are the restrictions of my kind."

Nessie nodded. She'd heard that about ghosts too. They could be stubborn and unhelpful, often verging towards riddles when they spoke. She was actually surprised at how many straight answers this one was giving them to start with. It went against everything she'd been told as a child.

"Thank you for sharing your wisdom with us." She dipped her head to Gilbert, hoping he took it as the sign of respect it was.

"And now you need to leave," the ghost said with a sad smile. "It's hard for me to keep up my human form. It's been a long time since I last spoke to another supernatural being. It makes it easier, yet it's been too long."

"Another..." Jonas repeated, then stared at Nessie. "I knew it!"

She instinctively took a step backwards until her back was against the cave wall. "I..." she stuttered. "I don't know what you mean." She turned to the ghost for help but Gilbert had already disappeared.

"You saw him," Jonas accused. "You lied to me!"

"I couldn't..." Nessie was lost for words. How could she explain to him without doing one of the worst sins she'd been taught? She couldn't expose her kind. She couldn't tell a human about the magical side of life. She just couldn't, her entire mind and body rebelled against the idea.

"I need to go," she stammered and stumbled out of the cave.

"Tell me!" Jonas shouted, following close behind her. He gripped her shoulders and turned her around until she was forced to look into his eyes. Rage shimmered in them, and disappointment. The latter hurt much more than his anger.

"Why didn't you tell me?" he asked angrily. "Why are you pretending not to know?"

Nessie fought herself free from his grip and began to run. It was all too much.

"You lied to me!" His voice was full of anger and anguish.

He was fast, but she was faster. She pushed some kelpie strength into her legs and ran down the path they'd taken to ascend the mountain. Wistfully, she realised she'd never actually stood on the very summit, but this wasn't the time. She'd return, one day, without Jonas. Without traitorous ghosts.

She almost slipped a few times on the scree, but she always managed to just about regain her balance. Soon, she was alone. Tears were running down her face even though she wasn't quite sure why. Maybe because she hated lying to the young man. Maybe because she'd wanted him to be her friend. Maybe because she was secretly lonely.

She stopped running when the rocky path entered the forest. What was she to do now? It seemed like it would be best to take her things and travel to the sea, just like she'd planned. And quickly, before Jonas had a chance to corner her. She knew he wasn't going to give up just like that. He'd had a taste of the supernatural now and all his theories had been confirmed. He was no longer going to believe that the legends were simple fairy tales. He was going to test every single myth he'd heard until he could prove whether it was true or not.

Secretly, she admired him for his conviction, but she couldn't help him. She had to get away from him before she spilt any secrets that would endanger her kind and others.

When did life become so complicated? Maybe staying in the Loch would have been better after all.

FIVE

She breathed a sigh of relief as soon as she was on the train west. Jonas hadn't appeared at the station as she'd feared. Now, she just needed to push him from her mind and focus on her mission: meet the sea kelpies and learn from them. Maybe meet a sea kelpie man and see if they were any better than Loch kelpie guys. Anything to get Jonas out of her mind.

This time, she had the compartment to herself for the entire journey. No more humans wiggling their way into her heart and thoughts.

She looked out of the window. The scenery was breathtaking. Cragged hills lined the rail track, small lochs and streams parted the moors into strange patterns. Greens of all shades painted the grass and mountains like an artist had wanted to try out every imaginable colour. It was so beautiful that her heart ached with a strange longing. She wanted to get off the train and walk through the highlands, soak in the atmosphere, but for now, she had to be content with simply enjoying the view.

When she got off at the train's final stop at Mallaig, all thoughts of Jonas had left her mind.

The little harbour town was full of people, most of them travelling onwards to the Isle of Skye. From here, she wasn't going to take human transportation, however. She was going to swim.

Before she left the village, she bought some chips at a small shop by the harbour. The woman looked at her a little strangely when she didn't take any fish, but kelpies were vegetarian. She only wanted the chips. They didn't have those underwater. Delicious, although the vinegar on them was an acquired taste. One she was planning to acquire by eating lots and lots of chips. But first, it was time to meet the sea kelpies.

She walked out of the village until she found a sheltered bay that was far enough away from the road so that she couldn't be seen by any humans. She quickly undressed and put her belongings back into her waterproof bag. It was getting a little full of the new clothes she'd bought, but she didn't want to leave them behind.

The water was cold but she loved it. Even though she'd only been away from her Loch for two nights, she realised that she'd missed the feeling of water on her skin. She waded in as far as she could without having to swim, then began the shift. When the pain got too much, she let herself drop underwater and screamed. Bones cracked as they lengthened and her skin tore as scales pushed through from underneath. It was high time that she met the sea kelpies and asked them if they really knew a painless way to shift. It seemed to be getting more painful each time.

Her lungs ached by the time her gills finally appeared on both sides of her neck and she could take a deep breath. It took a moment for her to regain full control of her body. She'd never been human for such a long time in one go. Suddenly, it was strange to have four legs and an antenna on her forehead. The sensations were a little overwhelming.

She grabbed her bag with her teeth and began to swim away from the shore. She didn't know where exactly the sea kelpies were living but she hoped her antenna was going to help with that. It sensed magic and there was going to be a lot of magic wherever the sea kelpies were. If they had the same kind of houses underwater as her kind did in the Loch, they'd be using magic to keep them in place, to keep the oxygen bubbles for visitors and kelpies who wanted to run around as humans. Kelpies were magical beings through and through, even though not all had the same kind of powers, nor the same amount of strength.

The water became colder the further she swam. Her Loch was the same temperature all year, but this was different. The salt was tickling her scales and she regretted having eaten salty chips before she left Mallaig. She was craving some sugar now to make up for it.

She swam a little further, noticing some telltale lights on the seabed. That looked promising, she just hoped it didn't belong to any merfolk. Not that she'd heard of any living off the coast of Scotland. As far as she knew, they preferred warmer climates where humans were more likely to be lured into the water by their song. The fishermen of Scotland had long since learned not to fall for their tricks. If they ever had in the first place. No. The real threat in Scotland came from the selkies.

A familiar string of clicks sounded in the water around her and relief filled every part of Nessie's being. Kelpies. There was no doubt that's what she was coming across. Though she couldn't see them, she could tell they were close and that they'd take her to their kingdom.

The clicks grew louder, calling out and asking who was there.

"I'm Vanessa, daughter of Meredith and Sherman," she clicked back, hoping they'd be able to hear her over the rush of the ocean. It was a lot louder here than when she was underwater in her own Loch.

No one responded to her introduction, but she didn't worry. She probably hadn't shouted loud enough and would just have to reintroduce herself when they came closer.

As suddenly as the clicks had appeared, grey shapes approached through the water, moving towards her in a formation she'd never encountered before.

"I'm Vanessa, daughter of Meredith and Sherman," she repeated her earlier clicks.

"We heard you the first time," one of the other kelpies, a male, clicked back.

"I'm here to..."

"Come with us," he cut her off.

Two kelpies closed in on either side of her, pushing up against her and steering her in the direction of the lights.

They were a little too close for her liking, but she'd put up with that if it meant they'd guide her to the safety of their home. The ocean was full of dangers she couldn't imagine and had never encountered before, an escort was actually kind of reassuring.

The city's bubble rose in front of them and the three of them passed through it easily, landing on the sandy bed and shifting back into their human forms. She hated this part. Her bones cracked as they shrunk and moved back into the right places. Her skin shredded and softened, leaving it with a raw sensation. But that was the price she paid for being able to change forms.

"Thank you for your escort. If you'd like to point me in the direction of..." She stopped talking as two cold manacles clamped around her wrists. "What's going on?" her voice shook as she tried to keep the fear out of them. One of the men picked up the waterproof bag she'd brought on her back and opened it, rifling through the meagre contents. He wouldn't find much. Just her clothing, a little bit of money, a diary, and the water bottle she'd taken up Ben Nevis but not used yet.

"You will be given a chance to speak at your trial. Until then, stay silent or risk being stopped from speaking," one of the men said as he snapped a third iron cuff around her neck.

Nessie shuddered, for the first time ever, she felt naked after a shift. She was so used to changing forms that nudity never bothered her. And yet now, it was almost too much for her to bear.

She didn't ask any other questions, too scared of what they'd do to her as a result. The last thing she wanted was for her adventure to turn even sourer than it had already.

The second man attached a chain to her collar and gave it a tug, forcing her to walk a few paces behind the two men as they set off through the city.

Other kelpies stopped what they were doing to stare at her as she passed. No matter, she wasn't just any kelpie, she would show them that she wasn't to be messed with. Nessie held her head high as she walked, keeping her hands relaxed and at her sides. Let them see her nakedness and know she wasn't ashamed. They could take what they wanted from here, but they wouldn't remove her dignity.

"Welcome to your new apartments," the first man sneered as he pushed her inside a cell.

More iron formed the bars of the prison, though she wasn't sure why. Iron had no effect on her other than being stronger than she was.

The cell door clanged shut behind her and the click of a lock stole all hopes of a quick escape. The second man sneered as he dropped her bag just out of reach on the other side of the bars. At least if she did manage to get out, she'd be able to take her things with her.

"Hands," he ordered.

She frowned, wondering what he wanted her to do with them. Deciding the only possible thing to do was to stick her bound hands through the bars, she did just that. The man came forward with a key and removed the manacles, letting them fall to the floor with a slight thud.

He smiled at her, sending a shiver down her spine. She hoped he wouldn't expect any alone time with her. She had no idea what he'd do if he did, but she did know it was best not to dwell on it too much. The man walked out of the door to the building, leaving her alone in the dark.

"I guess no one's removing the neck cuff then?" she muttered to herself.

Someone cackled behind her, almost making her jump out of her skin. "They won't do that, dear. It's to stop you from shifting."

Nessie turned slowly, unable to stop herself from touching the iron collar as she did. An old woman sat in the corner of the cell, a similar collar around her own neck.

"How do you..."

"One of the nicer guards told me when I asked if my own could be loosened. They chafe after a bit." She shrugged and looked up at Nessie. Glittering blue eyes cut through the dim light of the cell, showing a whole world of knowledge and experience behind them.

"Great." Nessie scuffed her foot against the floor, cursing herself for getting into this position. If she hadn't run away from Jonas and had told him the truth in the first place, then she wouldn't have been here. Then again, the sea and the kelpies under it had always been a part of her plan to explore.

"Where are you from?" the woman asked.

"Inland."

"Me too."

"How long have you been here?" Nessie asked, only a little worried about what the other woman might say.

"A year, maybe two. I was old already when I left my Loch. I was foolish in my youth and never left when I had the chance. Once my babies and grandbabies had grown, I decided it was my time to go and see the world. Now I guess I have." She gave a bitter laugh. "There's a lot of cruelty in this world, that's for sure."

"Why have they kept you here?"

"Who knows. They've never been particularly forthcoming on that front. I suspect they just don't like intruders in their territory." She shrugged again. "It's not so bad so long as you don't talk to the guards and do what they say. At least we get fed."

Nobody came to tell her what was going on. Nessie was fighting hard not to cry. She'd come to visit the sea kelpies to learn from them, to make friends, and instead, they'd degraded her and thrown her into a very medieval looking dungeon. It wasn't even one in the water, no, so she couldn't even be comforted by her kelpie form.

The old woman in the corner had fallen asleep and Nessie envied her. She would have loved to sleep, to dream herself away from this depressing situation. Less than ten hours ago, she'd been happy, carefree, enjoying the view from the top of Ben Nevis, and now here she was, a prisoner. If only her parents knew, they could get her out. They had good diplomatic relationships with the sea kelpies, at least that's what she'd heard. Had that changed? Had there been some kind of incident that had put them at war? Was she a hostage now?

If only someone came to tell her what was going on.

She rubbed her neck where her collar was beginning to painfully chafe against her skin. She didn't even try to shift; even if the collar wasn't preventing her, the lack of water would kill her instantly. She couldn't breathe air with her gills, she'd suffocate.

All in all, it was a desperate situation.

She wrapped her arms around her chest and waited for something to happen.

SIX

She lost count of the days. She was given food and water twice a day and once she was led to a shower room to clean herself. Besides that, she was left in the cell without any answers. On the second day, a guard gave her a simple dress that she gratefully put on, hiding her nakedness.

She learned that the old woman was called Mhairi, but besides telling stories of her grandchildren, the other prisoner wasn't giving up any information. She'd been in the cell for so long that she feared how a shift would feel. Maybe it would kill her.

"Nobody has ever tried to ransom me," she said as Nessie asked her for at least the tenth time. "And they haven't had any demands for me either. They just put me in this cell and left me like a discarded toy. But I've told you that before."

Yes, she had, but Nessie couldn't help but ask again and again. She still held a tiny spark of hope that there was a reason why the two of them were imprisoned at the bottom of the sea. It couldn't just be for the sea kelpies' amusement. They never even came to talk to them, so having prisoners for entertainment wasn't the answer.

Whenever the guards left, Nessie tried breaking open the lock. She'd searched the cell floor for a needle or a pin - not that she knew how to pick a lock - but there was nothing. Mhairi simply smiled patiently and watched as Nessie desperately searched for a way out.

While they were given enough food to sate them, Nessie was constantly hungry. Not for food, but for freedom. For social interaction. For stimulation of her senses. She'd never felt worse than how she was feeling now.

Footsteps in the distance made her look up from the sketch she'd drawn on the sandy floor. It was of a mountain; Ben Nevis. Two guards stopped in front of her cell, but instead of pushing two plates through the small opening at the bottom like they usually did, one of them pulled a key from his belt and opened the lock.

Immediately, Nessie was on her feet, hope beating in her chest.

"Hands," the other guard said and obediently, she held her arms out in front of her, waiting for them to attach the wrist cuffs. She felt as if she'd done something wrong, as if she was an evil person who deserved to be treated such, but then she remembered that she was just a young loch kelpie who'd gone in search of an adventure. She was innocent and she better hold on to that thought.

The guards led her out of the cell and up a flight of stairs. Nessie stumbled several times, weakness slowing her down more than the guards allowed.

"Where are you taking me?" she asked but there was no reply. Not that she'd thought that they'd tell her. It was just to fill the silence stretching out all around them.

After being pushed through several empty corridors, they finally entered a small room. Two male kelpies were standing at the other end of it, both dressed in fine clothes that made her think that those two might be the ones in charge.

"Leave us," the one on the left said with a deep, grinding voice. He was in his forties or early fifties, with grey strands peppering his otherwise black hair. He was wearing glasses, which was unusual for kelpies who rarely had problems with their eyes.

The other man was younger, maybe in his late

twenties and the complete opposite of the older man. He was blond, thin, and a smile was playing around his lips. He seemed much friendlier than the dark man.

The guards left Nessie standing in the centre of the room and closed the door behind them. She was alone with the two strangers and somehow, that made her feel scared. They could do anything to her, shackled and weak as she was.

"Vanessa, daughter of Meredith and Sherman," the older man said mockingly, repeating the words she'd spoken when she'd first arrived.

"Sherman, the betrayer," the young man hissed, the smile suddenly gone, replaced by a sneer.

"My father is no betrayer," Nessie shot back before she could stop herself. "I don't know what you're talking about!"

Even she could hear that her voice had a hysterical edge that betrayed her fear.

"I doubt that," the older man said, sarcasm lacing his words. "You wouldn't be here otherwise."

"I'm here to learn about the sea kelpies," Nessie said in desperation. It would be better to simply tell them the truth rather than come up with some kind of excuse. "I wanted to learn if you really have a way to make the shifting painless. And I wanted to see the world."

The blond man laughed. "And here you are,

admitting your guilt before we've even asked." He turned to the other man. "Is she really as stupid as she seems, Dactyl?"

She bit her lip, confused. She'd not admitted to anything, right?

"Sherman sends his own daughter as a spy," Dactyl muttered with a grin. "Yes, I believe the loch kelpies are as stupid as the stories say. My father was an idiot to have diplomatic relationships with them. We should have treated them like the inferior mutants that they are."

"Mutants?" Nessie gasped. "How dare you!"

She didn't care that she was a prisoner and at the two men's mercy. They'd insulted her and her father and she wasn't going to be quiet about that.

"Shifting isn't supposed to hurt," the younger man said in a bored voice. "It's just because of all your inbreeding that it has become that way."

Nessie was speechless. Inbreeding? Those men were going to pay for what they'd been doing to her. She hadn't figured out a way to escape and then punish them, but she was going to. She had to.

"How do you think so few kelpies can live in a loch and still keep having children?" the dark man asked.

"I don't know," she responded, shaking her head.

"Your people went inland to escape from the

fishermen. It's only become apparent that there were side effects now. Your father sought us out for our help and when we told him the truth, he refused to listen. Are you going to be the same, Vanessa, daughter of Meredith and Sherman?"

Nessie didn't know what to say. She wasn't the kind of kelpie to just give up like that and yet, what else was she going to do? He was talking about her family. Her people. To suggest they were all related...

"I'll listen," she said eventually, not seeing any other choice. Maybe if she listened to their tales, they'd even let her sleep somewhere that wasn't the hard cold cell floor when morning came.

"Good. Sit." The blond man indicated to a chair and she followed his instructions, not wanting to dare contradict him.

"What do you know about your own people and settling in the loch?" the dark man asked.

"Not much. We've been there for centuries as far as I know..."

"That much is true. The first kelpies travelled inland about five hundred years ago. They thought the water would be purer and the people around would be kinder. They were wrong. We never saw them again."

"And they settled in my loch?" Nessie asked.

He laughed deeply, clearly amused by her

assumption. "Not at all. Some roamed the land. Some started legends of their own. Some even mutated into something completely different. That's what happens over time. But most just died, sooner than they should have done too. And when the last one straggled home, he told us all tales of the world."

"And what tales they were," the blond added.

"Indeed. But no one else ventured out. For sixty kelpies had gone and only one had returned. Those are not odds the remaining kelpies fancied. Two hundred years later, another group braved the world above. The earth had changed and they found refuge in some of the lochs they found. There were five in total. Of those, three still exist, including yours."

She nodded. She knew of the other two lochs but had never been there. While she understood what they were saying, none of it really made sense of how it related to her father and what he'd done.

"We let the loch kelpies be, though of course, we knew from our own travels about how your biology had changed. The painful shifts and the lack of meat in the diet changed loch kelpies for good. They wouldn't survive here in the sea for longer than a year."

Nessie's eyes widened as the realisation of what that could mean sunk in. No one had told her that crucial piece of information when she'd set out into the world.

"But what has any of this to do with my father?" She couldn't imagine her kind and doting dad doing anything close to a betrayal of anyone.

"About forty years ago, a young kelpie came here. Your father. He was polite and adjusted to our ways quicker than we'd expected. Our sister was very taken with him. They spent a lot of time together. At first, we thought nothing of it. But then she told us she was in love and intended to return home with him when he went."

Nessie's mouth fell open. Reading between the lines, she knew what he was trying to say, she just wasn't ready to believe it.

"We told him no, of course," the blond said. "We couldn't have our sister taken away from us. She was the only daughter of the Empress of Kelpies. She was the only heir."

"And yet, she is not here," Dactyl put in.

"Are you saying..."

"That your father stole our sister from us?" Dactyl's eyes flared with anger, terrifying Nessie.

But his reaction also filled her with hope. If what this man was implying was true, then he was her uncle He wouldn't hurt her, would he? No one would do that to family. Even family they didn't know they had.

"My mother doesn't seem very stolen." Nessie's brow furrowed as she thought through every interaction she'd ever witnessed between her parents. There'd never been any kind of animosity between them. Far from it. There was no doubt at all that they loved each other heart and soul. As a young kelpie, she'd often dreamed of having a relationship like theirs.

"Whether or not she wanted to go with him, he stole her away from her people, her destiny. We are without an Empress and have been told by more than one prophet that we shan't have one for another hundred and twenty years."

"That's a long time."

"It's longer than either of us will see. Whether old age gets us, or the people who want an Empress," the blond said sadly.

"I'm sure that's not true..."

"I think you'll find it is."

"How can I convince you my father means no harm and I'm no spy?" She hoped they'd give her an answer, she had to return home and ask her parents some important questions. At least she was an only child, though that could change at any moment. Kelpies tended to be fertile up until the day they died and she was sure her parents would want another baby. In fact, she was surprised they hadn't already.

"You can swear an oath to us," Dactyl announced, a sly look in his eyes.

"Very well. What do you wish me to swear?"

"Repeat after me," he requested.

"Alright." She put her hand on her heart, ready to say whatever he needed from her.

"I, Vanesa, daughter of the traitor Sherman, and the true Empress of Kelpies, Meredith, do swear..."

"I, Vanessa, daughter of the traitor Sherman, and the true Empress of Kelpies, Meredith, do swear..." she repeated.

"...that my eldest daughter will be sent to the sea kelpies when she reaches the age of twenty-four, whereupon she will learn the ways of the true kelpies and take her rightful place as Empress of Kelpies."

"What?" Nessie blurted instead of repeating the words. Did they really expect her to swear away a daughter she didn't even have? Never to see her again or anything.

"You must swear it, or we shall get a daughter from you another way." Dactyl's tone left no room for arguments. She would have to do things his way.

All she could do was swear this now, and spend the years in between now and having a daughter to figure out how she could avoid forcing such a fate on the child.

"I swear that my eldest daughter will be sent to the sea kelpies when she reaches the age of twenty-four, whereupon she will learn the ways of the true kelpies and take her rightful place as Empress of Kelpies." She crossed her fingers behind her back as she swore, hoping she could uphold the promise to herself and find a way out of the oath. The last thing she wanted was any daughter of hers trapped under the sea for something she'd done.

SEVEN

Nessie was no longer a prisoner, but she also didn't feel like a guest. She was something in between. Guards followed her wherever she went and they made it very clear that they disapproved of her leaving her room. She could have left, but that went against her pride. She'd come here to find out more about the sea kelpies and she was going to complete her mission.

She wasn't allowed into the library, nor did any of the sea kelpies want to talk to her. Still, she decided she was going to be patient. Maybe if she could make some friends or at least non-enemies, they'd be able to help her.

She'd not seen Dactyl and Kell, the blond man, since swearing her oath. She was quite glad about that, although at the same time, she knew that they were holding the answers she was seeking. Sometimes, she wondered about the old woman who was likely still held in the dungeon. She'd tried to convince her guards to let her visit her, but they'd just looked at her as if she'd gone crazy. Maybe she had. Her instincts were telling her to run, to get as far away from the sea kelpies as possible, but she ignored them. Her curiosity was stronger.

After a week without progress, she decided she couldn't go on like this. Something had to change. She had no intention of spending the rest of her life down here with the sea kelpies. She missed her Loch and her family.

"I want to go for a swim," she told her guards. "To the surface. I need some proper air."

She'd been allowed to swim around the dwellings at the bottom of the sea, but she'd not seen the sun ever since she'd left Mallaig.

"I will have to clear that with our superiors," one of them said. He was the friendlier of the two, but they'd refused to give her their names. She called him Red due to his thick red beard. When he shifted, his scales had ruby shine. While he walked off, she was left alone with Surly Steve, her other guard. He rarely talked and when he did, he always sounded annoyed.

This time, however, he waited until Red was out of view, then pulled a thin book from under his uniform jacket.

"Maybe this will make you leave so we can go back to our normal jobs," he muttered under his breath and handed her the book.

Surprised, she looked at the cover. A watercolour kelpie was swimming in the sea, surrounded by small fish and even a few squids. *How to be a kelpie.* A children's book? He was actually giving her a children's book? Was he mocking her?

She prepared to give him an angry speech, but that's when Red came around the corner and she decided to hide the book in her bag. Even if Surly Steve was mocking her, she'd still keep the book to pass the lonely evenings. She'd had similar books as a child, but none of them featured sea kelpies.

"You're allowed to swim for an hour," Red said in his usual grumbly voice. "If you don't return by then, you won't be allowed back in."

It was clear from both the guards' expressions that they hoped she'd be late. They were fed up with being her babysitters just as she was fed up from being watched at all times. Maybe she should leave for good and go on the adventures she'd planned. See the world, meet *friendly* people, not be stuck inside glass domes deep beneath the sea.

"Fine," she snapped. "Let's go."

Without looking at them, she dropped her bag in her room - a clear sign that she did indeed intend to return - and headed to one of the changing rooms.

They were scattered all over the sea kelpies' homes, giving people a place to leave their clothes and belongings before heading out into the water. She undressed while her guards were standing behind her. Now that she was no longer wearing a collar and shackles, she didn't care about being naked in front of others. It was natural for her.

"One hour," Red repeated as she stepped towards the shimmering circle in the outer wall of the bubble.

Nessie nodded and grinned at him. "You won't get rid of me this easily."

He groaned but before he could say something, she took a deep breath and stepped through the magical barrier into the water. It was cold but she didn't have time to get used to the temperature. She focused on her kelpie form and pulled it towards the surface of her mind. Pain shot through her body as the shift began to take effect. It seemed even more painful than ever. Yet another reason to stick with the sea kelpies and find a way to prevent this pain.

When she was fully shifted, she swam to the surface as fast as she could. It was a beautiful day and the sunlight filtered through the water, turning into delicate beams reaching far down into the depths. Cool salty water was rushing through her gills and she greedily soaked up the oxygen. The webbing around her hooves gave her the extra push to propel her towards the surface. She whinnied happily, feeling freer than she had in a long time.

She began to swim faster, shooting through the waves. The sea was so much wilder than the Loch she'd grown up with and she loved the untamed energy of the water. The sound of the waves almost sounded like it was telling her stories, if only she'd stop and listen.

Nessie was so blissfully distracted that she never saw it coming. One second, she was happily clicking away in the kelpie tongue, the next she screamed in pain as something sharp embedded itself in her flank.

Panic filled her, overpowering the pain. She whirled around only to see the bottom of a fishing boat above her. She'd swam right into an arrow hook. How dare they! She wasn't a fish to be caught on a line!

Her human form seemed like a bad idea, but she couldn't let the humans see a shifted kelpie, even if it meant giving up any chance of getting back to the sea kelpies before the hour was up.

Cold air hit her drenched skin, causing her to erupt in goosebumps. Nessie stopped the struggle and collapsed against the side of the net, letting it carry the bulk of her weight. If they were going to catch her like a common fish, then she wasn't going to make life easy for them.

She crashed onto the deck, the impact making

her vision fail again. She sensed rather than saw the men crowding around her and wished she had the energy to cover herself. Forcing her eyes open, she looked up at them. There were four. Three blobs she'd never seen before and one who...

"You," Jonas hissed, his eyes narrowing in hatred.

"Me," she croaked, a small smile spreading across her lips.

"Throw her back overboard," the man said to the others.

"We can't..."

She strained her ears to catch the rest of what the men were saying, but couldn't make out a single word of it before blackness fell once more...

EIGHT

Warmth filled her senses. That didn't make any sense. She'd been underwater and the sea was undeniably cold, even for a kelpie.

Her eyes snapped open as the memories flooded back in. She'd been caught in a net. The sea kelpies would no doubt think she'd betrayed them just like they thought her father had. That couldn't end well for any of them.

"Ah, you're awake," a familiar voice said.

She turned her head, only half surprised to find Jonas looking down at her.

"What are you doing here?" she croaked.

"Funny story. After you ran away, I decided I was going to head to the sea anyway. I've heard stories about a ghost ship off the coast and wanted to try and press my luck to see if I could find it. The last thing I expected was to end up with you dragged out of the sea."

"It wasn't part of my plan either," Nessie muttered.

"I didn't think so. I told them you were my wife and I thought I'd lost you at sea. Luckily the people I was sailing with weren't the brightest and they believed me."

"Was?" The tense hadn't been lost on her. If he was talking in the past then it seemed likely they weren't at sea any longer.

"You were unconscious for a couple of days because you had a fever. We got back to shore yesterday so I booked us into a hotel and here we are." He shrugged.

"Thank you." She wouldn't have it said that she'd lost her manners while on land.

"You're welcome. Maybe you can repay me with some answers." He gave her a piercing look.

She nodded. At this point, he was more than aware of the existence of the supernatural world. Not to mention that he'd saved her life. There was no way around it. She owed him and if answers were all he wanted, then that was what he could have.

"Do you want something to eat?" he asked.

"Yes, please."

He gave her a weak smile. "I thought you might. I don't know what you like, so I got a bit of everything." He gestured towards a small table laden with food.

"Thank you. Anything without meat is good," she told him.

"What about seafood?"

"Definite pass."

"Okay, bread and cheese it is." He walked over to the table and loaded a plate with all kinds of food, bringing it back to her and passing it over.

"Thank you." One look told her it was more than *just* bread and cheese like he'd implied, and she dug in, feeling her strength returning with each bite.

"So, are you ready to tell me what you are?"

"Who's to say I'm anything?" she responded through bites of food.

"I find it unlikely that anyone could survive in the sea for that long without being something more than human."

"Fair point."

"Are you another ghost?" he asked.

She shook her head vigorously. "I'm very much alive."

"Good to know. I was starting to worry I was afflicted with necrophilia," he said under his breath, probably not intending for her to have heard it.

She spat out the bread she'd been eating. "I'm sorry, what?"

"You heard that?" A panicked look crossed his face. "Your hearing must be impeccable."

She shrugged. It was true that her hearing was better than that of a human, but he hadn't been that subtle about it. She wondered where the attraction between them had come from. Especially as it seemed like a mutual thing. She'd never really been interested in kelpie boys. Maybe it was because she'd known them all her whole life rather than meeting them when she was mature herself. Or maybe it was more than that. Gilbert had mentioned fate and she couldn't ignore the implication that maybe there was more to life than just going through each day. And if it was fate, who was she to deny it.

"Are you going to tell me what you are?" he said eventually.

"I'm a kelpie," she admitted softly.

The look on his face said it all. He'd heard tales about her kind and now he wasn't going to be able to look at her ever again. Something sank like a rock in her stomach. She hated the idea of him not looking at her. It was the last thing she wanted.

"Okay." He breathed in slowly, clearly trying to work out what to do next.

He rose to his feet and removed his jacket, hanging it over the back of a chair before rolling his sleeves up and revealing taught skin over well-formed muscles. All the adventuring was surely paying off.

Nessie licked her lips before reminding herself he'd just discovered what she was and probably wasn't thinking about her in that way. Nor would he ever. Much to her annoyance.

He didn't say a word as he headed towards one of the doors leaving the room. As soon as he opened it, she let out a sigh of relief. He was only heading into the bathroom and not away from her completely. If he abandoned her in the hotel, she'd have no way of even paying for it now she didn't have her things any more.

Running water reached her ears, soothing her in some way. When he didn't reappear after a few moments, Nessie's curiosity got the better of her. She swung her legs out of bed, noting then that she wasn't naked any more. Maybe she should feel embarrassed that Jonas had seen her naked but it didn't seem important in the grand scheme of things.

She padded over to the bathroom door, peering around and gasping as she took in the naked torso of the man leaning over the tub. As much as she wanted to study the broad set of his shoulders and the rippling muscles as he moved, something else had caught her attention...

"The bath isn't quite ready for you yet," he said, not turning to look at her.

"Bath?" She frowned, not understanding what he meant.

"If you're a kelpie, then you need water."

She stared at his back, not knowing how to respond to that properly. "Thank you."

"You're welcome." He stretched down into the tub, probably to test the temperature, drawing her gaze back to the thing that had her so confused.

"Where did you get that mark?" she asked, staring at the familiar symbol tattooed on his back.

"What mark?" He looked over his shoulder, a frown marring his features.

"The one on your lower back." She could have sworn she'd seen the Celtic symbol for water there.

"I don't have a mark on my lower back." There was no mistaking his confusion for anything other than what it was.

Feeling daring, she stepped forward and traced the lines with her fingers. He stilled under her touch, hopefully enjoying the connection as much as she did. "This one," she whispered.

"Mirror," he demanded and she handed him a small hand mirror from the sideboard.

"I've got a tattoo," he muttered in shock. "Like a sailor."

"What's that?" Nessie asked in confusion. Why was he suddenly comparing himself to a sailor?

"It's a permanent painting on your skin. The ink gets pushed under the skin with needles. It's not something people like me usually get."

Gently, she ran a finger over the mark. "It's beautiful," she reassured him. "If I ever get a tattoo, it would be like this."

He smiled at her. "It's not something ladies do."

Nessie shrugged. "I'm not a lady. At least not a human one. I may look human, but I'm kelpie."

Jonas nodded and turned off the tap after once again testing the water temperature. Nessie was still stunned by his thoughtfulness. Instead of running away screaming like she'd expected - after all, the common belief was that kelpies ate humans - he'd immediately thought of her needs. And all that after she'd lied to him and run away.

"Am I doing the right thing?" he suddenly asked. "I've never met a kelpie before." He grinned at her. "Obviously."

She nodded. "I don't need to go into the water regularly to survive, but I don't feel well without it. It's like my skin permanently itches. Now that I've been away from the sea for a few days, I'm going to enjoy the feeling of water on my body."

A blush reddened Jonas's cheeks. "I'll leave you to it. But maybe... if I sit on the other side of the door, maybe you could tell me about the kelpies?"

Nessie laughed. "I'm not bothered by nudity," she explained when she saw his questioning look. "When we shift, we're naked, so it's not a big deal for kelpies."

"Oh," he muttered. "So I can stay here with you?"

Suddenly, heat spread through Nessie as she thought of the consequences of her words. Usually, she didn't mind anyone seeing her naked and it was normal for her to feel indifferent about it, but why was she growing so excited at the thought of Jonas watching her while she was taking a bath? What was so different about him?

"Yes," she replied, her voice shaking a tiny bit. To cover her insecurity, she turned and pretended to test the water temperature. Not that it mattered. Kelpies were quite resistant to both hot and cold. Staying with her back to Jonas, she took off her clothes as fast as possible. His breathing got quicker. Was that because of her? Was he afraid of her now?

Slowly, she turned around, meeting his heated gaze. There was something in his eyes that she couldn't identify, but she loved the way he looked at her. His eyes flickered up and down her body, then focused on her face again. His cheeks got even redder when she smiled at him. She was tempted to ask whether he liked the view, but that would have been a little too forward. Her insides were on fire as she stared at his upper body, the hard muscles that begged to be touched.

She tore her eyes away from him and stepped into

the bathtub. Immediately, the itching on her skin ceased and a pleasant tingle took its place. The same tingle she'd felt when she'd touched Jonas. Was there some kind of new magic going on between the two of them? This wasn't normal. And now the mark on his back.

"Where do kelpies come from?" Jonas asked, sitting on the floor and leaning against the wall, his long legs spread out in front of him.

Nessie tried not to think about how amazing he looked like that and focused instead on the question. "There's a colony in the sea, and a few in some of the lochs around Scotland," she answered honestly, trying not to think about the new truths she'd learned about kelpie-kind. That was just going to start her down a path she wasn't sure she was quite ready for.

"And you can just walk on land?"

"Pretty much. We actually spend most of our time in human form. Our homes are buildings much like yours here, except that they're underwater."

"But you do have another form?"

"Yes."

"What does it look like?" His eyes lit up as he asked.

"A bit like a horse? I guess. But we have an antenna coming from our foreheads, scales, and webbed hooves."

"I'm sure you look formidable," he said full of excitement. "What's the antenna for?"

"It's like an additional sense that detects magic. It's not very important in everyday life though. All of us use magic and there's no need for us to sense it."

He gasped. "You can do magic?"

Oh. Seemed she hadn't mentioned that part.

She smiled at his stunned expression. "Yes, most of us can. The majority of kelpies have water-related powers, but some of us can influence other elements. My uncle has the gift of foresight while my father can lift things with his mind alone."

"That's incredible!"

Nessie smiled. It was cute to see his child-like wonder. For her, it was normal. That's why she'd always found humans a little boring. They couldn't do magic, they couldn't shift, they couldn't do anything. How did they even survive without becoming depressed?

"And what's your power?" Jonas asked.

She grinned. "Let me show you. Take a look at the water."

He shifted closer and peeked over the rim of the bathtub. Suddenly, Nessie was very aware of her nakedness again. He could see everything through the clear water. Every tiny bit of skin. She was bare before him and for some reason, that excited her. Just like before, tingles raced through her, making the hairs on her skin stand up straight. She'd always found it weird how she had hairs on her arms and legs but scales all over her body when she was shifted. Did her hair turn into scales? Or did it just disappear and then regrow from scratch?

Jonas cleared his throat and she shoved those thoughts from her mind. It was time to show off.

She reached for her magic and formed a single, large drop of water in the air, hovering above the palm of her hand. Jonas gasped again, but she'd only just started. She made the drop expand until it was the size of an apple. It began to spin around its own axis, faster and faster until the light shining on it turned into a miniature rainbow. It had taken her a long time to have this much control. It was easy to throw a large amount of water at enemies - or annoying friends - but it was much harder to keep control of just one or two drops. They were slippery and her magic tended to squash them before she got a chance to play with them. This time, however, it worked out perfectly.

Nessie brought the drop to a standstill and then made it split in two, looking just like something cut it in half, with a smooth straight surface on both of the newly formed drops. She made some more water rising up from the tub, forming a wall in between the two drops.

"Do you know the tale of the two Royal

children?" Nessie asked softly, not taking her eyes off her work.

"No," Jonas muttered, transfixed.

"They were in love but they couldn't get to each other." She made the two drops wiggle a little, making them look like they were trying to get through the wall.

"So one of them lit a candle that the other could follow, leading them together. There was some conspiracy with an old nun who blew out the candle and all that, but let's just imagine that it worked."

She squeezed one of the drops through the water wall and made it hug the other drop until they became on large blob once again.

Jonas laughed. "Do you usually change fairytales to suit yourself?"

She shrugged. "It would have taken forever had I included all the court intrigue."

Nessie released her magic and the drops fell back into the tub, ending the spectacle.

"That was beautiful," Jonas said, his eyes wide. Then he added, quieter this time, "Just like you."

Had he just made her a compliment? And was she supposed to reply to it? Tell him how beautiful he was? Was that how humans did it? Or anyone, in general? She didn't have much experience in this area.

"I like your muscles," she whispered and to her horror, he started laughing.

"No one's ever told me that before," he chuckled. "Women usually aren't that forward."

Nessie refused to feel embarrassed. "I'm not other women. I like your muscles and I'll tell it how it is."

His grin turned into a gentle smile. "That's why I like you. I know we only just met, but even from the moment we first spoke, I've known that you're different. You understand me and my desire to learn more about the world. Although right now, all I want to explore is you."

A pleasant shiver ran through her. His words were beautiful, resonating deep within her. She was melting beneath his gaze. If she wasn't careful, she'd succumb to his charm. But then, why would she resist?

Before she even knew what was happening, he leaned over the rim of the tub and cupped her face with his warm hands, drawing her near until their faces were so close she could feel his hot breath on her cheeks. His lips hovered above hers and for a second, she wondered whether he'd retreat, but then he pressed his mouth on hers, gently kissing her.

She'd kissed men before but she'd never felt this many emotions while doing so. She wrapped her arms around his neck, hoping he wouldn't mind that she was dripping wet. His fingers drew through her hair, his thumbs drawing circles just beneath her ears.

None of that was as intense as his lips though. His warm, soft lips that were full of promises and unspoken words. She gasped and opened her mouth as the tip of his tongue gently ran over her bottom lip. She quivered and was glad that she was sitting, otherwise her legs may have given in. Warmth was spreading between her legs that had nothing to do with the water she was bathing in. How did his kiss have such an effect on her? It was just a kiss. Just the mechanics of her lips on his, but... his tongue invaded her mouth and all thought fled. She moaned, unable to stop herself. He gripped her harder as if he was afraid that she might run like she had back on Ben Nevis. Now she wished she hadn't. She'd missed out on a month's worth of kisses.

Tentatively, she brushed her tongue against his. When he groaned, she continued her exploration. What had he said? He wanted to explore her? Right now, she wanted to do just the same to him. She'd never been with a man, not fully, but now it was the only thing on her mind.

She ran her hands down his back, admiring how she could feel the hard muscles beneath his skin. She'd never asked what he did for a living, but it had to involve physical work. Or maybe he'd been born as an Adonis.

When her fingers reached the hem of his trousers, he groaned again. He stopped the kiss for a moment to whisper, "Are you sure you're not a succubus?"

Then, without warning, he wrapped his arms around her waist and pulled her out of the bath until she was pressed against his chest. She hadn't seen that coming, but as much as she loved being in the water, for once she was very happy to be out of it. Very happy.

"I'm a kelpie," she replied, her mouth seeking his to continue what they'd started. "Otherwise you'd be undressed already."

He chuckled, the sound vibrating against her skin in an oh so pleasant way. She could get used to this. It wasn't anything like when she'd been with other men. They didn't understand the effect they could have on women.

Jonas hoisted her into his arms, his strong arms under her legs and back, supporting her in a way she wouldn't have expected. he carried her back to the bed and lay her down before stepping back.

"You truly are beautiful." His eyes raked down her body, leaving a trail of warmth in their path.

"You're not so bad yourself." A short giggle escaped as she finished speaking. She would have been shocked over how out of character it was for her if the situation had been any different. "But you're wearing far too many clothes still."

He chuckled again. "It does seem like they're

getting in the way." His hands rested on his belt and he had it off seconds later, sending his trousers falling to the floor and revealing himself to her.

Now she understood why some kelpies preferred their lovers to be human. He was certainly impressive down there.

"Are you sure you want to do this?" he asked, concern flitting across his face.

She nodded eagerly and reached out for him to join her on the bed. "This isn't my first time," she admitted.

His eyebrows raised but he came to the bed anyway, sitting beside her and trailing his hand down her arm. The tingles intensified and she had to wonder if this was a human thing or just a Jonas thing.

"Is virginity not a prized thing where you come from?"

"Not particularly. Is it here?"

"Seeing a woman's ankles is seen as scandalous here."

"I'm sorry, what?" She tried not to laugh, but the mere notion was ridiculous. Why would seeing ankles be a scandal? Though she supposed it was different for humans. They didn't get naked nearly as often as kelpies did.

"Ankles are the height of scandal. If you're

showing them to a man, you better be prepared to marry him," he warned.

"Was that a proposal?" she murmured, reaching out with one hand and cupping his cheek, hoping he'd take the hint and kiss her again.

"I..."

"It's okay, there's no need to explain, I understand what this means." Though she still hoped it would turn into more, even if she had no idea how a human-kelpie relationship would work. Maybe this would be enough to stop the sea kelpies from wanting her first daughter though. Surely a hybrid would be no use to them at all.

She pushed the notion away just as Jonas's lips pressed against hers. She melted into him, eager to give all of herself to him and experience what he had to offer. Something told her she'd never be able to go back to sleeping with the male kelpies back home after this.

He shifted in the bed so he was hovering over her, the heat radiating off his body hard for her to ignore. Not that she wanted to. The closer they got to the final moment between them, the more she needed it. She just hoped he'd still be around in the morning. There was so much more she wanted to explore with him, especially now he knew the secret she'd been hiding.

Nessie arched up, pushing her body into his and

feeling yet more tingles as their naked skin met. There was no doubting the intensity of the attraction between them and no denying the call of his body to hers.

He trailed his fingers up the inside of her leg, dancing over the soft skin of her thighs. Nessie moaned into his mouth, urging him on without having to speak the words. He didn't need them either. His fingers moved higher still, coming to rest between their bodies and mere inches from the spot she longed for him to touch.

"Are you sure?" he whispered against her lips.

"Yes," she answered, her breathing already laboured and he hadn't even touched her properly yet. As sweet as it was that he kept checking she was comfortable with the situation, she just wanted him to move on to the next part of their adventure together.

Thankfully, he didn't ask again. Instead, he pushed his fingers into her, causing a groan to escape from her lips and fill the room.

"More," she murmured, not wanting him to think he was causing her any pain and stop. That would be the worst way for this to end.

He chuckled against her skin but didn't say a word. Instead, he kissed her neck, before moving down her body with a string of small kisses and nips.

Nessie wriggled against the bed, desperate to get more from him.

Jonas settled between her legs. Their eyes met as he looked up her body, his wicked smile taking all of her attention. She'd heard about what he was about to do, but none of the kelpies she'd been with had done it. Anticipation thrummed through her as he kissed the inside of her thigh.

Letting her legs fall open further, she invited him in, even as his fingers moved inside her, hitting the spot within her that she couldn't ignore. His tongue darted out, pressing against her most sensitive parts and jolting her from the bed with a long, loud, moan.

He hummed, sending more vibrations through her, pleasure coiling in her belly and urging to be released.

"More, please more," she begged.

Jonas chuckled but pulled back from her. She didn't mind though, she knew what was coming next and couldn't wait to feel him inside her, no doubt driving her even crazier than he already had been.

He nudged at her entrance, no longer asking for reassurances about the permission she'd already willingly given. With one strong thrust, he seated himself inside, nearly sending her over the edge. She pushed into him, desperate to be closer than anyone thought possible.

They writhed together, each lost in the sensation of their bodies coming together. Moans slipped from Nessie's mouth, completely unstoppable even if she'd wanted to. She arched up into him, gasping for breath. She knew it wouldn't be long until she fell over the edge.

As if sensing her thought, something rumbled through her, flooding her senses. A crest of pleasure rose within her, mimicking a tidal wave in its intensity. It crashed through her, causing her to shudder uncontrollably. She was dimly aware of Jonas groaning in her ear, but she couldn't focus on that with so much pleasure coursing through her.

Riding out the wave, the two of them collapsed back onto the bed. Nessie's mind turned to sleep now she was sated, even if she hadn't been awake that long. Jonas seemed just as zoned out but pulled her into his arms, holding her tight and pulling her into blissful sleep.

NINE

They enjoyed the bathtub so much that it took them two days until one of them left the hotel room, and that was only to get some food. Luckily, Jonas had bought enough supplies to last them for a bit, but all their physical exercise - Nessie snickered at that thought - made them hungrier than usual.

She now knew Jonas's body inside and out. They'd explored each other, they'd talked for hours on end, then they'd ended up in bed again. Or on the floor. Or in the bathtub again. Nessie was sore in places she hadn't even imagined to ever feel sore in, but it was a good kind of pain. It reminded her of what they'd done and what they would repeat very soon. Both of them were insatiable. And for a human, Jonas really had a lot of stamina.

"Penny for your thoughts," the man in question

said, chuckling slightly when it took her a moment to become fully aware of him. She'd been lost in thought, reminiscing over his body and the way he felt when he moved within her.

"Ehm... I was thinking that I should really try and talk to the sea kelpies again," she stuttered, not wanting to give him the satisfaction that he was all she was really thinking of just now. "I still want to know if there's a painless way for me to shift and they said they have one. Problem is, I don't think they're going to let me in, or they might even arrest me again."

Jonas frowned. "I'm not letting you put yourself in danger. Is there no other way to learn that shifting method? A book perhaps?"

Nessie remembered the children's book one of the guards had given her. It was a long shot, but maybe there really was something in there that might help.

She sat up from the bed and smiled. "Get dressed. We're going shopping."

They found a small bookshop in an alleyway that seemed forgotten by most passerbys. It was dimly lit and smelled distinctly of old paper and dusty corners.

"Hello?" Nessie asked as they entered. The

shelves were stacked to the very top with books and her immediate thought was that they were going to need help finding what they were looking for. If there was some kind of order to the way the books were sorted, she didn't see it.

An old man appeared from behind a shelf. He perfectly matched the shop's old-fashioned interior. Perhaps he was part of the furniture, as they say.

"How can I help you, dearie?"

His voice was soft and pleasant, reminding her of an evening by the fireside. She frowned. Where did that image suddenly come from? And why was she feeling warm, like she was sitting in front of hot flames?

"I'm looking for a children's book," Nessie said, a little hesitantly. Hopefully, he'd believe that she was buying the book for her nieces or nephews. She was a little young to have her own children. Kelpies rarely gave birth until they were in their late twenties. They were fertile for longer than humans, which made sense, they lived longer than them after all.

"I think it's called *How to be a Kelpie*."

The man smiled. "I've not sold one of those for years! But I believe I still have a few in the back, let me check."

He shuffled off, leaving Jonas and Nessie waiting. He immediately walked over to one of the shelves and pulled out a few books, beginning to read one of them.

"I didn't think there was a sequel," he muttered and Nessie left him to it. She knew how distracted book lovers could get. She was one herself, although she'd not got used to the feeling of human paper books yet. The ones they had down in the Loch were etched on kelp, making them waterproof.

"I found one!" the old man called out from the other side of the shop, triumphantly waving a familiar book. When he handed it to her, he lowered his voice and winked at her. "Is it for yourself?"

Nessie wanted to lie, tell him that it was for her non-existent niece, but something in his eyes made her hesitate. They were blue, so blue that they seemed unnatural, for a human at least. There was a thin golden circle surrounding his pupils, reminding her of the eyes of the sea kelpies. Maybe he had kelpie blood in his family.

"Yes," she nodded after a moment. "I'm very interested in kelpies."

That was vague enough that it could be interpreted as an academic interest.

"You're not from around here," the man observed. "It may not help you. This book is about sea kelpies."

"Are there different kinds of kelpies?" Nessie asked innocently, testing the old man.

He smiled. "I think you already know the answer to that."

Jonas appeared behind her, handing the man two books and waving his wallet.

"Four pounds for those," the man told Jonas before turning back to Nessie. "And you can have yours for free, dearie. But as I said, I think you'll be disappointed."

When they left the shop, they headed to a cute little cafe around the corner, giving them the chance to read the kelpie book right away. Over a cup of tea, they perused the illustrated pages. The text was simple and short, aimed at children, and covered the life of kelpies at sea. There was barely any mention of kelpies also having human forms; all the drawings were of shifted kelpies swimming around the sea. There were no illustrations of the underwater domes, strange considering that both the sea and the Loch kelpies had those.

On the last two pages, the book finally mentioned shifting.

"Kelpies are able to shed their horse-like skin and become human like you and me," Nessie read aloud. "They can do that because they're full of magic. You might think that changing from a horse into a human hurts, but that's not the case for kelpies. They are born with the ability to be both and shifting is as painless as putting on new clothes."

Nessie huffed. "Not for me, it isn't."

"They're full of magic," Jonas repeated. "That suggests that the way they shift is natural, they don't need to learn how to do it. Was that the same for you?"

She shook her head. "It took me several months to learn how to do it properly. At first, I only managed a partial shift. Turning my scales into human skin was the hardest. Kelpie parents can somehow make their children shift, so I knew how it was supposed to feel, but doing it myself was so much harder."

Jonas frowned. "Your parents can make you shift? Does that hurt?"

"No, it's completely painless." Nessie gasped. "Maybe that's it! Our parents still have that magic the book talks about, the one that helps you shift without pain, but it only works to help their children. We must have lost the ability to use it on ourselves."

Maybe the sea kelpies had been right. They were mutants, their skills hampered by being away from their original kin for too long.

Sadness and disappointment threatened to overwhelm her. "I'm never going to be able to shift without pain," she muttered. "It's all been for nothing."

Jonas reached over the table and squeezed her

hand. "I wouldn't say that. You wouldn't have met me if you hadn't set out to visit the sea kelpies."

She stayed quiet, mulling over what she'd just read. Jonas was sipping his tea, aimlessly flicking through the pages of one of the books he'd bought.

"How..." he suddenly whispered and hastily put his teacup down. "I didn't buy that one."

"Huh?" Nessie asked, only half paying attention.

Jonas held up a thin, old book. "I only bought two books but now I have three. This one wasn't there before."

Nessie frowned. "Maybe you picked it up by accident?"

He shook his head. "No, I'm sure I only handed him two books when I paid. He must have slipped it between them. But why?"

"What's it called?" Nessie asked, unable to read the title upside down.

"The Seven Wardens."

TEN

She turned the page again, sure the symbol would change between this time looking at it and last time. And yet, there it was. Standing on the page just as clearly as the mark on Jonas's back. The only difference between his symbol and the one in the book was that this one was surrounded by six more marks. One for each of the Wardens.

"Remind me what it says about the markings?" Jonas was pacing back and forth, his sleeves rolled up to his elbows.

"The leader of the Wardens will be marked seven times, each one appearing as he or she melds their powers with the other Wardens. This can be done in person, or in an alternative plane but must be done before the Wardens can fulfill their duty and create a stable world once more," she read.

He ran a hand over his face, messing up his hair in a delicious way that reminded her of the time they'd spent together in bed. Nessie knew she had to push that from her mind though, they had bigger things to focus on.

"Right. And the other six Wardens are?"

"It doesn't say. They could be anyone from anywhere in the world." She closed the book with a sharp snap. It wasn't like they didn't already know the damn thing by heart. When it was the only thing standing between them and answers, there was no other way.

"And I'm one of the Wardens?" His voice was filled with something complicated, though she couldn't tell if it was excitement or dread. Either would be appropriate given the situation.

"My guess is that you're the Water Warden. Your proximity to the sea probably sparked something in your body to make the mark appear." Either that, or it was something to do with her, but she felt it was better not to say that out loud to him. Not yet, anyway. Maybe later when they were more in control of everything.

He sighed and sat down on the bed. "I guess there was always a reason why I was so interested in the supernatural."

Nessie reached out and stroked his back, hoping the move was as soothing as she intended it to be.

"I'm sorry I dragged you into this world," she whispered.

"We both know that when fate comes calling, it's nothing to do with the company we keep," he pointed out with a short laugh. "You're not the reason I'm a Warden, just a catalyst to me finding out I was one."

She didn't say anything. She knew he was right but was too concerned about him blaming her for this to consider anything else. Now she'd found someone like him, she never wanted to let him go. Not when she had an opportunity to be happier than she'd ever thought possible.

"If you'll let me, I can come with you? The book said that often Wardens had companions who helped them on the journey, even if they weren't Wardens themselves." She said the words so quietly that it was hard to tell if he'd actually heard or not, especially as the silence stretched between them.

"Don't you need to carry on your quest for painless shifting?"

She breathed a sigh of relief, glad he wasn't outright telling her no. That was a start, even if it was a very slow one. "I don't think I'm ever going to get to the bottom of that one. The pain doesn't stop us from shifting, it just makes it hurt a little. Once the shift is done, it's over."

"Will I ever see your shifted form?"

"Yes," she whispered after studying him closely for a moment. She had no idea how he'd react to seeing her in her other form, especially when it wasn't conventionally pretty. But she knew she wanted to trust him with that part of herself. She wanted to trust him with every part of herself, even if she wasn't going to be able to do certain things like take him home to the other kelpies. If what she'd learned was true, she was already a hybrid, adding a human into the mix as a potential father to her children was sure to muddy the waters, even if her family were high up the food chain.

"Thank you." He leaned over and placed a hand over hers, giving it a quick squeeze. "But what do we do now?"

"I guess the only thing we can do is find the other six Wardens," she responded. "Even if only you have made yourself known at the moment, it must mean that the supernatural powers like the Staran need the Wardens to help steady them."

"Why aren't the previous Wardens still doing it?" he asked.

She sighed. She'd kept that part of the book from him on purpose, but maybe she shouldn't have. "Being a Warden will prolong your life and youth, but you will still die. The previous seven Wardens must be all dead by now."

Contrary to what she expected, his eyes lit up at

that. "I'm going to live longer?" he asked and she nodded. She'd thought she'd told him but he'd either not fully understood or she'd imagined it.

"Yes, you'll live at least a few decades longer than your fellow humans."

A smile began to make his face even more beautiful. "That means I'll live long enough to be with you."

Warmth filled her chest and she returned his smile. She wasn't going to tell him that she would likely still outlive him, but he was right, his new lengthened lifespan would give them more time together. They could have a life. Marriage. Children. Grandchildren, even. She gave herself a mental shove. No, she couldn't think that far ahead. First, they needed to figure out this Warden thing. The mark appearing on Jonas's skin had to mean that something important was happening. The Wardens were needed and she was going to support Jonas every step of the way. Just because she wasn't a Warden herself didn't mean she couldn't get involved. She loved meddling.

Jonas got up from his chair and walked around the table, halting in front of Nessie. She looked at him in confusion as he went down on one knee. What in water's name was he doing?

"Miss Nessie," he began, his voice serious. "Would you do me the honour of going on a quest with me?"

She laughed. She couldn't help it. Him looking all

serious while asking her such a ridiculous question was too much. This day had been full of revelations and disappointments and it all culminated in this strange, surreal moment.

Jonas frowned, taken aback. He seemed disappointed with her reaction. Had she done something wrong? Was this some sort of human ritual?

Suddenly, there was clapping behind her and she jumped up from her chair, even more confused. An elderly couple in the corner were clapping, smiling widely at her and Jonas.

"Did she say yes?" the older man called out while his wife grinned at Nessie.

"She's not answered yet," Jonas muttered, a blush creeping up his cheeks.

"Say yes!" the woman encouraged her loudly. "Don't let the poor boy wait."

Frowning, Nessie met Jonas's eyes. What was going on?

"Say yes," he whispered, giving her a cheeky wink.

Well, it wasn't as if he'd asked her something really life-changing. Going on a quest with him sounded fun. If it turned out to be catastrophic for some reason, she could always leave.

She smiled at him indulgently.

"Yes."

More clapping all around the cafe, this time even the waitresses were applauding her.

She looked at Jonas for help.

He simply grinned.

Humans were strange, and somehow, she had the impression that she'd said yes to much more than just a quest.

EPILOGUE

Many years later

The final battle had been fought and won, but at a terrible cost. The Seven Wardens were no longer. They'd died to save the world.

Nessie wished they hadn't. Screw the world, screw the Warden's sense of duty.

"You weren't supposed to die," she told the gravestone in front of her. "You still had so many years to live."

She gently brushed over the smooth marble stone, removing a tiny leaf that had landed there. He was buried by the sea, his gravestone looking out over the waves. He'd loved that view. When they built their house not far from here, he'd always talked about building a bench right here on the cliff. Now, he never would. For a moment, Nessie considered doing it herself, but that didn't feel right. Besides, she was returning to the Loch, the place where she'd grown up.

She wasn't going to bring up her daughter by herself. She just couldn't. Not when every time she looked into her baby's eyes she saw Jonas looking back at her. She had his eyes. The man she'd loved, the only man she'd ever wanted to be with. Before she gave birth to her daughter, she'd been able to travel to a strange in-between place where the dead Wardens were waiting for the next generation. Jonas was only a ghost there, unable to touch her, but she'd been able to talk to him. Now though, ever since her daughter had arrived, she was no longer able to access that place. She'd never had the chance to say goodbye.

"You stupid, stupid man," she muttered, hoping he'd somehow be able to hear her from that other place. "Why did you have to go and die?"

She didn't expect an answer but suddenly, the wind around her turned warm, almost like a hug. She leaned into it, imagining Jonas's strong arms holding her, just like he always used to when she was upset. She missed him so much.

"You mustn't tell her," the wind whispered into her ear. She shrieked, swirling around, but there was nobody there. She was alone on the cliff, the gravestone her only companion.

"She needs to grow up away from the Warden legacy," the disembodied voice continued. "Keep her father a secret." It didn't sound like Jonas, but there was a certain familiarity. Some kind of friendly spirit aiding the Wardens, perhaps?

"Why?" Nessie demanded. "How can I not tell my daughter about her father? She will ask questions."

"It's necessary. You will understand once she comes of age. She has an important role to play and she won't be able to do it if she already knows the price Wardens have to pay. She needs to be protected until she's ready."

"Ready for what?" Nessie shouted, anger bubbling up in her. Someone was messing with her daughter's fate, even though she was only a baby.

"You need to trust me. I know it's hard but she can't know she's your child. Give her to your younger sister."

Tears began running down Nessie's cheeks. This had to be a joke. No, a dream. How could any mother abandon her child?

"Who are you?" she screamed. "Why should I trust you?"

The wind sighed. "Miss Nessie," it whispered, stroking her tear-streaked cheeks. "Would you do me the honour of going on a quest with me?"

Her knees gave in and she fell to the ground.

"No," she whimpered. "I can't."

"If your daughter doesn't become who she's meant to be, the world will end. So will the Wardens. Your daughter will die. Our deaths will have been for nothing. We will never meet again in the afterlife. Can you really risk all that?"

Pain tore through Nessie's heart. Give her child to her sister? Not be the mother she'd imagined to be? She scrambled up to her feet and ran back to the house, not stopping until she held her daughter in her arms. The baby was sleeping peacefully, not waking even when Nessie pressed her against her chest.

"I love you," she whispered. "You'll always be mine. I will look after you, little one, and I'll always be there, watching out for you. Even if you don't know it."

The baby opened her eyes. Jonas's eyes. That only made more tears run down Nessie's face. She almost couldn't bear it.

"I will be your Aunt Nessie," she promised amidst sobs. "I will make sure you have the best life imaginable. And when the time is ripe, I will tell you. I will tell you everything. About your father. How he died. How he lived. And how he loved me. And how he loved you, even though he never got to see you."

She smiled sadly. "And then you're going to save

the world. Macey, my girl, saving the world just like your father did."

She pressed a kiss on the baby's forehead.

"I'll always be there for you, even if you don't know why."

The baby smiled at her as if to say that it was alright. That she was strong enough to deal with the lies that Nessie would have to weave to keep her daughter safe.

So be it.

Thank you for reading Beyond the Loch! This is only the start of the great adventure though... Nessie is a big part of her daughter Macey's journey in the Seven Wardens series, a paranormal reverse harem drenched in Scottish mythology. If you enjoyed this story, take a look at the Seven Wardens books:

skyemackinnon.com/sevenwardens

Subscribe to our newsletters:

skyemackinnon.com/newsletter

authorlauragreenwood.co.uk/mailing-list-signup

- Inside the Egg (novella set after the events of the Seven Wardens series)
- Seven Wardens Boxed Set: Books 1-4
- Seven Wardens Boxed Set: Books 5-7

ABOUT LAURA GREENWOOD

Laura is a USA Today Bestselling Author of paranormal, fantasy, and urban fantasy romance (though she can occasionally be found writing contemporary romance). When she's not writing, she drinks a lot of tea, tries to resist French macarons, and works towards a diploma in Egyptology. She lives in the UK, where most of her books are set.

Follow the Author

- Website: www.authorlauragreenwood.co.uk
- Mailing List: www.authorlauragreenwood.co.uk/p/mailing-list-sign-up.html
- Facebook Group: http://facebook.com/groups/theparanormalcouncil
- Facebook Page: http://facebook.com/authorlauragreenwood
- Bookbub: www.bookbub.com/authors/laura-greenwood

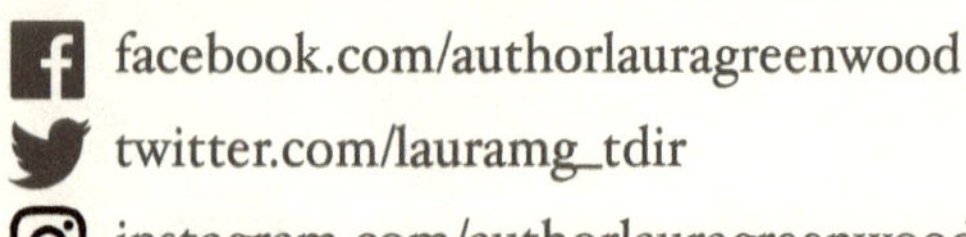

facebook.com/authorlauragreenwood

twitter.com/lauramg_tdir

instagram.com/authorlauragreenwood

bookbub.com/authors/laura-greenwood

amazon.com/author/lauragreenwood

ABOUT SKYE MACKINNON

Skye MacKinnon is a USA Today & International Bestselling Author whose books are filled with strong heroines who don't have to choose.

She embraces her Scottishness with fantastical Scottish settings and a dash of mythology, no matter if she's writing about Celtic gods, cat shifters, or the streets of Edinburgh.

When she's not typing away at her favourite cafe, Skye loves dried mango, as much exotic tea as she can squeeze into her cupboards, and being covered in pet hair by her demon cat Sootie.

Subscribe to her newsletter:
skyemackinnon.com/newsletter

Join her Facebook group:
facebook.com/groups/skyesbookharem

facebook.com/skyemackinnonauthor

twitter.com/skye_mackinnon

instagram.com/skyemackinnonauthor

bookbub.com/authors/skye-mackinnon

goodreads.com/SkyeMacKinnon

amazon.com/author/skye_mackinnon